A SUMMER SONG

Love was the melody she never expected to hear

BARBARA MCMAHON

A Summer Song
Copyright © 2010,2025 Barbara McMahon
All Rights Reserved

Chapter One

Angelica Cannon stepped off the bus into another world. Dragging her heavy backpack down the steps, she made sure she did not let the precious violin case hit anything. The air was thick with heat and humidity, sultry and hot. The trees that lined the street offered scant shade with the sun directly overhead, but gave some illusion of cool, dashed by the reflecting heat from the asphalt.

Running away wasn't as easy as she'd thought when she stuffed things into her backpack and left without telling a soul where she was headed. Withdrawing a hefty sum from her bank account, before buying a bus ticket south, she was officially off the grid. She'd pay cash for everything and defy anyone to find her before she was ready.

She didn't expect to be stepping into another world. Maybe— just maybe—she'd bit off more than she could chew.

Three pairs of eyes watched her disembark from the old bus. Two men had to be close to eighty, their scant gray hair covering little of their heads, their overalls looking as if they'd been made during the Great Depression. They sat on rocking chairs, but were still, as if watching people get off the bus was too important to miss by rocking back and forth.

The third set of eyes latched onto hers and for a moment she caught her breath, unable to step away from the bus, unable to breathe. The man leaned casually against one of the posts holding the roof above the wide porch. His stance was decidedly male.

Dark and dangerous, his eyes reflected that image perfectly. His black hair was wavy and longer than the men she normally associated with. He could be the grandson of the other two, as he couldn't be much over thirty. Buff and brawny—she almost swallowed her tongue as she stared at him, consumed by the spark in his eyes, the way he let his gaze move slowly over her then snap back to hold her eyes in that compelling stare.

Her heart sped up. Her sophisticated veneer shattered. She'd never felt such an instant raw sensual attraction before. It was as if every cell in her body became attuned to his. And she hadn't a clue who he was.

She took a breath and, conscious of someone waiting behind her, stepped away from the bus—toward the trio on the porch of the rough-hewn building that served as bus station, general store and gas station. And a place for old men to watch the world go by. A place for a man to mesmerize with his stare.

Wide shoulders, muscular arms and chest, nothing was hidden by the skintight navy T-shirt he wore. Faded jeans over motorcycle boots covered long legs. His face was all angles and planes, tanned a dark teak.

She'd never seen anything as gorgeous in her life. The fluttering feelings inside kicked up a notch and she wished she could check makeup, hair and clothes. And find something scintillating to say that would impress him with her wit and sophistication.

Clothes—darn. She looked down at her outfit. The two of them almost matched. She wore a cotton top and faded jeans. So unlike her normal attire. In fact, she'd bet her mother didn't even know she owned a pair of jeans.

Not that she was going to think about her mother! The great escape included thoughts about her parents, her job, and where she was going in the future.

"You miss your stop, sugar?" the man asked as she approached the porch.

Attuned to musical pitch and tone, Angelica almost swooned with the deep baritone voice and sweet Southern drawl. Talk some more, she almost said. Instead, she replied,

"Is this Smoky Hollow, Kentucky?"

"Last I heard," he acknowledged.

"Pretty thing," one of the older men said, as if she weren't standing six feet in front of him.

"Why's she here? Kin of anyone we know?" the other asked.

"Just fixing to ask that myself."

The fascinating man stepped off the porch in a casual and utterly masculine manner that had Angelica wondering if her hormones had spiked in some weird way since crossing the state line. She wanted to step up and flirt.

Flirt? She had never done so in her life. Where was that thought coming from?

"Can I help you?" he asked. "I'm Kirk Devon and I know almost everybody around here. Who're you here to see?"

She blinked. His *heah* didn't quite sound like *here* did at home.

"I'm looking for Webb Francis Muldoon," she said.

He tilted his head slightly, his eyes intent on her face.

"Webb Francis isn't here," he said.

She swallowed. Great, she left home and fled fifteen hundred miles and the man she was running to wasn't even around. A second of uncertainty surfaced. Then she took a breath, needing more information. She wasn't going to be stopped at the first setback. She had yearned for this for too long.

"When will he be back?" she asked.

"Don't rightly know. Might be a few days. Maybe longer. What do you want with Webb Francis?"

He took a step closer and Angelica wanted to step back. He was tall, at least several inches over six feet. Next to her own five and a half feet height, he seemed to tower over her. But it wasn't only that. Tapered waist and hips, long legs and those broad shoulders made him look as if he could carry the weight of the world easily on those shoulders. Strong and masculine in an earthy way she wasn't used to. She was fascinated, and overwhelmed. Her senses roiled.

"I prefer to explain that to Mr. Muldoon," she said stiffly.

The bus door clanged shut and the old bus belched a puff of black smoke as it pulled away and groaned down the street.

Angelica watched it go, then looked back at the man in front of her. His eyes were still intent, studying her every expression.

"Looks like your transportation's gone and left you here. Webb Francis is in hospital at Bryceville. He has pneumonia."

"He's sick?"

Professor Simmons had assured her she'd be welcomed by Webb Francis. No one had counted on his illness. Least of all her.

"Friend of yours?" Kirk Devon asked still studying her.

"He's a friend of—a friend."

She closed her mouth without saying another word. She dare not trust anyone. She wasn't giving out who she was or why she was there until she'd spoken to Webb Francis to see if this was where she belonged. She gazed after the bus. Where was Bryceville? Would the bus have taken her there?

"Got a place to stay?" Kirk asked.

She shook her head slowly. She'd thought Webb Francis would help her by recommending a place to stay. She knew

Professor Simmons had written a letter for his old friend explaining everything. It was in her backpack, to be given once she met Mr. Muldoon. Looking around she squared her shoulders. She'd traveled in Europe, called Manhattan home, surely she could handle one small town in Kentucky.

"Any hotels around?"

She'd have seen one as they'd approached, watching as she had the foreign scenery as the bus drove in from Lexington. No skyscrapers here. But maybe there'd be a small boutique hotel on a side street.

"There's a B&B in town. Sally Ann's place.She probably has room. You can stay there tonight, decide what to do tomorrow. Don't reckon Webb Francis will be home before a week. And not then unless folks rally around. He'll need care. You staying long?"

He stepped closer, almost crowding her. Reaching for her violin case, he offered to take it. She snatched it out of his reach, stepped back and swung slightly around so the case was almost behind her.

"I can manage. Just point me in the right direction."

His dark eyes watched for a moment. The air was charged with tension, then he gave a lopsided smile and relaxed.

It was harder for Angelica to adjust to the change. The smile caused crazy feelings. He was probably a harmless guy trying to help. But she didn't feel reassured.

He was big and strong and too sexy for her own good. She couldn't get beyond that attraction. His dark hair almost shimmered with streaks of blue, it was so black. When he smiled, she felt a catch in her heart. He could probably charm the birds from the tree with a single smile.

She was not a bird. She had to remember she had a goal and falling prey to the first good-looking man she saw was so not in her plans.

Reseating her backpack on her shoulders, she glared at him. No one touched the valuable violin but her.

"I'll take your backpack, then," he said, lifting it from her shoulders before she knew it. "Can't let a lady carry all those heavy things," he drawled as he turned and gestured for her to proceed in the direction to the left.

The sidewalk ended fifty feet beyond the store. The road narrowed, feeling closed in with the trees that flanked it on both sides. With the sun overhead, there was little shade to ease the heat reflecting from the asphalt. If she'd had any idea of how hot it was in Kentucky in summer, she'd have—done what?

This was her only bolt hole and she was grateful for it. She'd have to deal with the heat. She hoped the walk to the B&B wasn't long, or she'd be a melted puddle in the road. Glancing at her companion, she was annoyed he didn't seem to notice the heat at all.

If his pace was any indication, it didn't bother him at all. She was growing winded.

"You didn't tell me your name," he commented after a few yards.

"Angelica Cannon."

She felt sure no one around here had ever heard of her. It was as if she'd stepped into a time warp, looking around at the lack of amenities and action. Circa 1900, she thought. She felt curiously free knowing people here would only learn what she chose to share about her life. She could be totally anonymous if she wanted.

"Sally Ann runs a B&B, you said?" she asked.

The shoulder was gravel and dirt and not wide enough to walk on. Would it be any cooler if she could take to the dirt instead of the asphalt? She was growing grateful to her guide that he'd taken the backpack. She was so hot!

"She does. And makes the best pancakes this side of the Mississippi. You tell her you want some one morning and she'll pile them on your plate. You look like you need some good down-home cooking."

Angelica frowned. Was that a backhanded comment about her slender frame? Or an insult? Did he think women needed more curves to be attractive?

What did she care? He was some backwoods guy, not one of the men of influence she was used to dating. Not a patron of the arts, not a subscriber to the symphony. He probably wouldn't recognize genuine world class music if it hit him on the head.

His longer gait had her rushing to keep up. Not that she'd ask for him to slow down. That'd only prolong her listening to the slow Southern drawl and risk forgetting any good sense remaining.

Though how dashing away in the night showed good sense, she wasn't sure. She hadn't been a prisoner. She should have stayed and shown the logic of her choices.

Only, she still couldn't envision herself standing up against her parents. They had done so much for her. They only wanted the very best. How ungrateful she'd be to rail against everything.

And it wasn't as if she was turning her back on her life. For the most part she enjoyed music. It was only lately—she needed a break. She was flat-out burned out.

Try as she might, they never listened to her. Always pushing, always saying they knew what was best for her. She was almost twenty-eight years old. Surely she had to know what was best for her by now.

Coming here without confirming her would be host was available didn't show such good sense—even she had to admit that. But she had come and now she'd make the most of whatever chance she found. It was only temporary. Worst case, she could relax for a few days and then make new plans.

Through the trees she caught a glimpse of a large white clapboard structure. As they rounded a slight bend in the road, Angelica saw the house straight-on. A bit shabby in appearance, nevertheless it was impressive, with a wide porch, dormer windows flanked by green shutters and an immaculate green lawn. Flowering bushes encircled the base of the house. A colorful flower plot in the center of the lawn surrounded an old oak tree whose shade was just starting to touch the wide front porch of the house. Rocking chairs and benches lined up in a row.

Did every building in Smoky Hollow have a porch? She'd heard Southerners were laid back group. It had to be the heat. She'd like to lie down until the temperature dropped about twenty degrees. Maybe sitting in the shade was the next best thing.

Kirk stepped on the porch and banged on a screen door. The wooden door to the house stood open wide and a moment later a woman bustled down the hall that stretched out from the door, wiping her hands on a dish towel.

"Kirk, gracious, good to see you. Is there something wrong?"

"Hey Sally Ann. I brought you a paying guest."

"I declare."

She opened the screen door and stepped out, looking at Angelica with curiosity.

"Was I expecting you?" she asked, tilting her head slightly and smiling.

She tucked the dish towel in the top of her apron.

Angelica shook her head.

"Mr. Devon said you might have room. I came to see Webb Francis Muldoon and learned he's not here."

"No, poor man, sick as can be in Bryceville. Mae went over this morning to see him. Evelyn and Paul will be going tomorrow. When are you going back, Kirk?"

"Might take this young lady to see him tomorrow if that's what she wants," he said, flicking a glance at Angelica.

Angelica studied him for a moment. Her common sense told her to stay away from this man. She could forget her own name if she wasn't careful. Yet if he offered transportation she'd take it.

With her expected ally gone, she needed to reassess everything. How long would Webb Francis be sick? What was she to do in the meantime?

"I'd pay for the ride to Bryceville," she said looking straight at Kirk.

His face pulled into a frown.

"Not if I'm going that way anyway. I'll leave around ten. Meet me at the store."

He turned and gave Sally Ann a wide smile.

"You take care of this one. She's not used to Kentucky."

He handed Angelica the backpack.

Angelica couldn't argue the point, but she wondered how obvious she appeared. She felt like a stranger on a different planet. Glass and concrete canyons shadowed by tall buildings was her milieu. The breeze blowing from the Hudson. Or freezing winters fighting slush and traffic and time.

Her reluctant guide turned and began walking back the way they'd came.

"Thank you," she called, ever mindful of manners her mother had drummed into her head.

He didn't acknowledge her appreciation.

"He can't hear you," Sally Ann said. "Come on in. I've got a nice room right on the front of the house. Gets the breeze at night. Quiet, too, unless those Slade boys are carrying on."

Angelica nodded and followed her hostess into the house, wondering who the Slade boys were and what carrying on meant.

The tall ceilings kept the temperature tolerable. It was a relief to be out of the sun. Climbing stairs that creaked with each step, she wondered how old the house was. The faded wallpaper on the walls gave the feeling of days gone by—long gone by. But the house was spotlessly clean. And smelled like apple pie.

"Here it is. What do you think?"

Sally Ann stepped into a large room with wide windows overlooking the street. The oak tree in front shaded it from the sun. It wasn't as cool as air-conditioning could achieve, but it was pleasant enough. Definitely twenty or more degrees cooler than outside.

The double bed was covered with an old quilt. There was a slipper chair near one of the windows, a large double-wide bureau and knickknacks galore from little ceramic kittens playing with yarn to old figurines of ladies in antebellum attire.

"This is nice," Angelica said, taking it all in.

It was vastly different from her sleek Manhattan apartment, with chrome and leather furnishings and modern art on the walls. This was warm and homey. She'd never seen a place like it. She liked it.

"Supper's at six. If you don't eat here, there's a good diner in town. Which isn't too far a walk. Without a car, you're going to be hard-pressed to find anything else you can walk to and get back before dark."

"I'd like supper here," Angelica said, slowly lowering her backpack to the floor.

Her precious violin she hugged against her chest for comfort. She felt it was the only familiar thing in life right now.

"Meals are extra." Sally Ann quoted a figure that was ridiculously low.

Angelica smiled and nodded.

"I'd like that."

If everything was that cheap in Kentucky, she could stay longer than originally planned.

If Webb Francis got well and agreed to help her.

And if she could keep her mind on work and not the disturbing presence of Kirk Devon.

Kirk planned to call Webb Francis as soon as he reached a phone. Did the man know Angelica Cannon? He hadn't seemed worried about an invited guest showing up when Kirk saw him yesterday.

The more he thought about it, the odder it seemed. What would a young woman whom no one ever heard of have in common with Webb Francis—except for the fiddle. Webb Francis was a world-class fiddle player. At the music festivals and hootenannies held in and around Smoky Hollow, Webb Francis was renowned for his talent. Could she be a student wannabe? That would explain the violin case she guarded.

Melvin and Paul still held the fort on the porch of the store. There were a couple of others from town chatting with them. Waiting. When they spotted Kirk, the questions began to fly as everyone wanted to know more about the woman who came to visit Webb Francis.

"I don't know any more than you do. I'm taking her over to see him tomorrow. Maybe that'll clear things up."

He spoke another minute or two to the neighbors then headed for home. It was hot. Late July in Kentucky was always hot. He'd been in hotter places. But a long time ago. Time and places he didn't want to remember.

Next time he'd take his motorcycle. It wasn't a long walk to town, but midday wasn't the time to be out walking in the sun.

Reaching the log cabin built as if it grew directly from the forest floor, Kirk went straight to his phone. In a moment he was connected to Webb Francis at the hospital.

"You expecting an Angelica Cannon?" Kirk asked after ascertaining his friend was improving.

"Who?"

"Some woman with a fiddle in a case, backpack, faded jeans and a secretive attitude."

"It doesn't sound like anyone I know. Far as I can remember, no one's going to show up to see me."

"Claims she was expecting to see you. I figure she's going to try to talk you into giving her some lessons or something."

Webb Francis coughed for a long moment. Then said, "I'm not up to that. Send her on her way."

"I'm bringing her in to see you tomorrow."

"I'm not up to taking on a student. The doctors here can't even tell me when I'm going home."

"Rest up. We'll sort this out tomorrow. She's staying at Sally Ann's tonight. If you're not up to seeing her, she can come back after you get well. Need anything?"

Webb Francis coughed again.

"Naw, I'm good. It'll be good to see you, Kirk. I don't know about some stranger."

"Take it easy. I'll handle things."

"You always do. Good thing for me and your granddad you came home when you did."

Kirk stared out the window at the bank of trees. Good and bad. If he hadn't returned, he could believe Alice was waiting for him.

Still—his grandfather needed him. He'd seen the sights he'd wanted to see. It had been time to return home.

"See you tomorrow," he said and slowly hung up the phone.

Action kept memories at bay. He rose and went to the studio behind his house. He could get in some serious work this afternoon. And evening. And maybe think a bit more about the stranger who looked sad and lost and a bit scared.

She presented a puzzle. Strangers didn't come to Smoky Hollow often. Faded jeans and cotton top could be clothes of anyone. But her porcelain complexion and wide, tired blue eyes spoke of something different. Who had such creamy white skin these days? Her blond hair had been pulled back into a ponytail at the nape of her neck, sleek and shiny. What would it look like loose in a bank of waves framing her face?

He shook his head. He didn't need interest rising at this juncture. He knew enough to know whatever her story, she wouldn't be long in Smoky Hollow. And he'd had enough trouble with women in the past. Something had always been missing. He didn't think about it any more. He liked his life just the way it was now. No complications, no drama.

And a tad lonely.

He pushed away the thought when he entered the structure a short distance behind his house. He'd built both buildings himself, using the knowledge and skill he'd picked up from many construction projects over the years. From the outside, both the house and shed merely looked like log cabins. Inside he had utilized the finer aspects of carpentry that enabled the house to be comfortable and stylish.

The studio was a different matter. With strongly insulated walls, it was cool in summer, warm in winter, and totally utilitarian.

Standing in the doorway, he flipped on the switch. The daylight fixtures bathed the entire space in plenty of light. The tall windows added natural daylight. In the center of the building stood the sculptured piece of wood he was currently working. Five feet tall, it was not quite life-size. A mother with a baby in her arms and a child clinging to her knee, the semi-abstract rendition gave the illusion of motherhood everywhere without details to features and age.

The carving part was finished. He walked around it, studying it from every angle. Next was the final stage—sanding until it was as smooth as glass. Then applying the stain that would bring out the natural luster of the wood. Bring the statue to life. He reached for the first sandpaper and began long even strokes down the length of the back.

Caught up in his work, he didn't realize the passage of time until he felt the pangs of hunger. Glancing at his watch, he realized it was after midnight. He hadn't eaten since lunch. Time to take a break. He placed the staining cloth in an airtight container, put the used sandpaper in the trash.

Studying the figure once more, he was pleased. The deep stain had highlighted the grain of the wood. The smooth finish was pleasing to touch. He knew Bianca would snap it up for her gallery. He'd take photos tomorrow to send to her. Once they agreed on price, he'd load it up and deliver.

It was cooler than expected when he stepped outside. He walked the familiar path from his studio to home with out light. He knew every inch of his property—and most of the surrounding properties as well. Another way to keep the memories at bay, walk in the dark where he could become attuned with nature, and forget the curve balls life some times threw.

Chapter Two

Angelica arrived at the store several minutes before ten the next morning. The two older men she'd seen yesterday were both in the same spot. Had they spent the night there?

"Good mornin'," one said.

"Morning, miss," the other echoed.

She greeted them both and then turned to look down the road. She hadn't a clue in which direction Kirk would come from. Probably not from the B&B as he had walked back toward the store when he left yesterday. She hoped he'd meant it when he offered her a ride. She hadn't a clue how to get to Bryceville on her own.

"Nice day," one of the men said.

"Beautiful," she agreed.

Then took a moment to really appreciate the morning. It was already warm, but not as hot as it had been yesterday. The tall trees were widespread, shading a good portion of the store and parking lot. She could hear birds trilling in the branches. She tried to remember the last time she'd noticed birds singing in the morning.

She rarely opened the windows in her high-rise apartment. And when she did, it was traffic noise she heard, not birds. Her parents' home in Boston had huge elm trees in the yard, yet she couldn't remember ever listening to birds.

How odd. Was she normally oblivious to what was going on around her?

A low rumble sounded to her left and she looked that way. In only a moment a motorcycle roared into view, stopping when it reached the porch. The throaty purr of the engine filled the morning air. Taking off his helmet, the driver grinned at her.

"Ready to go to Bryceville?" Kirk asked.

She stared at him and at the big black-and-chrome motorcycle, fear and fascination warring.

"On that?" she almost squeaked.

She'd never ridden a motorcycle in her life. What if it crashed? She flexed her fingers. What if she spilled onto the pavement and damaged her hands?

"I have an extra helmet," he said, unstrapping it from the back and holding it out to her.

Angelica stared at it for a moment. She looked into his eyes which seemed to challenge her. The seconds ticked by. No one spoke. Only the trilling of the birds filled the silence. Almost fatalistically she stepped off the porch.

She had deliberately come here. She'd wanted something different and found it—in spades.

Hesitating another moment, she took the helmet, put it on. Then, following his instructions, she climbed behind on the powerful motorcycle. Once seated, she felt the vibration beneath her, the warmth of the man in front of her.

"Hold on," he said, putting his own helmet back on.

When she hesitated, he reached back and brought both her arms around his waist, slapping one hand over the other. It was impersonal and expeditious.

That move brought her slam up against his back. She felt every muscle as he pushed the bike back from the porch. She didn't view it as impersonal, this was very personal. Her body against his, her arms around his hard stomach. She couldn't breathe. Her blood pounded through her veins.

He gave the two old men a wave. In seconds they were flying down the narrow country road.

Angelica caught her breath in fear, closed her eyes and tightened her grip on the one solid thing in her world right now, Kirk Devon. His entire body seemed rock solid. His stomach muscles were like iron. His back muscular and hard. Once she caught a breath again, she risked opening her eyes. She slowly rested against his back, head turned sideways. She lifted her head and peered over his shoulder. Trees whipped by. The black pavement seemed to unfold like a ribbon before them, curving and twisting, opening up straight ahead for long stretches before diving back into the thickness of the trees.

Gradually the fear morphed into elation. She felt as if they teetered on the brink of disaster, yet Kirk seemed to know exactly what he was doing. If this was his normal mode of transportation, he was an expert.

She couldn't ease back on her desperate hold, but she could breathe again. And slowly begin to relish the wind racing across her skin, seeping into the helmet. She wondered what it would be like to fly along without the safety helmet.

Fear faded. He hadn't crashed, no reason to think he would with her onboard.

Conversation was impossible. Which was a good thing. She couldn't think of a single topic of conversation that might interest him.

She could hardly ask out of the blue if he were married. She shouldn't be so aware of another woman's husband. Her curiosity spiked. Had he always lived in Smoky Hollow? What did he do for a living? He hadn't been working yesterday. And obviously wasn't working this morning. Did he have rotating days or something? Was this his weekend? Or was he visiting like she was?

No, he'd known those men on the porch. Known Sally Ann. So what was a guy as dynamic as he was doing in sleepy Smoky Hollow, Kentucky?

Maybe he was unemployed. Lot of that going around.

She could consider herself unemployed. Her last contract had ended and she had yet to sign the new one waiting for her at her agent's office. She had enough in savings to live quite a while before she needed to find another position. Inevitably, she'd return to New York. What else could she do besides play the violin?

She hoped by then, however, that she'd know herself better and be able to withstand the pressure placed on her by others. This was her first vacation ever. She'd gone right to the symphony from the conservatory. Toured Europe when the New York season ended.

She needed this break, and hopefully the new direction it'd give her.

Today was too awesome to have to consider the future. It was enough to take delight in this moment.

After being plastered to Kirk's solid back for the better part of thirty minutes, Angelica was reluctant to move when they reached the hospital.

He sat for a second after he stopped and then said, "It's safe to let go now."

Burning with embarrassment, she snatched her hands back and awkwardly got off the motorcycle unassisted, almost falling on her face. His arm caught her around the waist while she was still trying to get her legs to move.

Heart aflutter, knees wobbly, she pulled back and took off the helmet. She slicked her hands over her hair; it still felt in place. Tied back as it was, it didn't get mussed often. Though she'd never worn a helmet before.

He took both helmets and placed them on the handlebars. Then headed for the hospital entry.

"Are they safe here?" she asked, glancing back at the motorcycle in the parking lot.

"Sure." He shrugged. "If someone needs them more than I do, let him take them. I can buy others."

She'd never thought about that aspect of theft.

"What if they just want to resell for money?"

"As I said, if they need it more than I do, okay by me."

She followed, trying to understand his thought process. Where she lived everyone was out to get ahead, to be the brightest and best, to make more money, to protect what they'd acquired. Now this man seemed totally unconcerned about the safety of his equipment.

Entering the hospital, Kirk guided her to the elevator and they rose to the third floor. Angelica kept her face forward, denying herself the opportunity to gaze at Kirk Devon. She hoped he had no idea of how edgy she felt around him—so aware of herself as a woman and him as a man. She wasn't some teenager. Even thought it almost felt like she was with a crush on the cutest guy around.

Maybe Webb Francis would be well soon enough to help her. If not, she wasn't sure what she'd do. Having made the break, she didn't want to return home without having accomplished her goal.

But she hadn't a clue what she could do in Smoky Hollow waiting for him to recover.

There seemed to be a lot of bustle in the corridor leading to

Webb Francis's room, with doctors jotting notes on charts, nurses checking on patients. Kirk walked confidently along and knocked perfunctorily on the partially opened door.

Entering right behind him, Angelica saw the older man propped up in bed with an oxygen cannula in his nose. His white hair was brushed back from his face. He looked pale and wan to her eyes. He smiled when he saw Kirk, then looked pleasantly curious when he saw her.

"You brought her, I see," Webb Francis said.

Kirk offered his hand and gripped the sick man's briefly, then turned to look at Angelica.

"Angelica Cannon, meet Webb Francis Muldoon."

"Hello, Mr. Muldoon. I'm sorry to learn you're ill. Professor Simmons suggested I come to see you."

She pulled out the letter the professor had written on her behalf.

"This explains things, I hope."

Webb Francis took the letter. He read it through then looked at Angelica.

"Miss Cannon, I'm honored you'd come to learn from me. Seems like I could learn from you."

"Please, call me Angelica. I've had a rather narrow focus lately. I want a change. My favorite class at the Conservatory was folk music. I'd love to hear it firsthand and put some effort into learning the music."

The memory of her parents' rejection of her suggestion she follow up with more folk music classes back in her student days flickered. She pushed it away. She was old enough to be in charge of her own life and the direction she wanted to go.

"Ah, a good project. Sorry you found me laid up, eh, Kirk?"

Kirk shrugged.

"If you say so. What's the latest from your doctor?"

While the man responded, Angelica watched the interaction. Kirk had the habit of focusing entirely on the person speaking. He didn't let any distractions enter in. She liked that. It beat someone always looking at his watch, or scanning the surroundings to be noticed, to scope out who else might be around.

"The man says I'm not going to be released until my blood gases are back to normal. Then I need some in-home care. Told him I'm feeling better and I've been taking care of myself for a long time," Webb Francis said.

"Everyone needs a hand from time to time. That's easily taken care of," Kirk said. "Just let me know when to come get you."

"Still gonna be a few days."

Webb Francis tapped the refolded letter against the sheets. He studied her for a moment, then said, "Angelica, you could stay in my house until I get back. Save B&B expenses at Sally Ann's. I got a couple of empty bedrooms. Pick the one you like. When I'm better, we can discuss what I can or can't do for you."

She flicked a glance at Kirk. What would he think of his friend offering the use of his house to a virtual stranger?

From his frown, Kirk wasn't in favor of the idea. But he said nothing.

"When you come home, maybe I could help," she said.

She'd love to learn as much as she could from the man. Until he returned home, she'd talk to some of the residents of Smoky Hollow. From what her professor had said, folk music was well represented in the hamlets of Kentucky.

"We'll see."

The older man looked at Kirk then Angelica.

"Show her around for me, Kirk, will you? And introduce her to Dottie and Tommy. They know lots of the old songs. Tommy plays the dulcimer, you know. And Gina. She'll be a help."

Kirk hesitated a moment, then shrugged and nodded.

"Did you come on Kirk's motorcycle?" Webb Francis asked Angelica.

She nodded.

"First time I've ever been on one," she confided.

Kirk grinned. "Best way to see Kentucky," he said.

It must be a private joke because Webb Francis laughed at Kirk's comment.

"You take care of my guest until I get there, you here? Show her around. Make sure she has everything she needs."

"I hear. I'll make sure she gets the royal treatment."

He looked at her while he said it.

Angelica felt every cell in her body come to attention. She wasn't sure she liked that idea. She'd rather not spend much time around this disturbing man. She'd never felt this strong attraction before.

Most of her dates had been with men more interested in being seen with a rising star than in developing deep personal relationships. Not that she dated much. Schooling and then practice had taken a huge priority in her life. She wasn't comfortable about her reaction to Kirk. Hopefully it would fade in the next ten minutes—or sooner.

The two men chatted for a few minutes. She stepped back and watched, fascinated by the peek into their lives through their conversation about people they both knew. Most of her friends were musicians. From the comments made, Webb Francis and Kirk had a wide assortment of friends. She listened wistfully, fascinated.

"What about the music festival?" Webb Francis asked at one point.

"It'll all come together," Kirk said.

The topic piqued Angelica's interest.

"What music festival?" she asked.

"The last weekend of August we have a big musical festival with folks coming from all over the state. We play, sing, dance. That's one event you don't want to miss," Webb Francis said. "There'll be a couple of impromptu gatherings before then, I expect. Rehearsals of a kind, jam session mostly. Usually happens throughout the summer. Kirk, see what you can get going. Then Angelica can play for us."

Kirk nodded, looking at her.

"Play that fiddle you carry around, huh?"

"It's a violin. A very old and valuable one," she said with some asperity. A fiddle indeed.

"Same thing," Webb Francis said. "I've got some sheet music in the little room off the living room. Find you some music so you can play at the festival," he suggested.

She nodded, annoyed Kirk seemed amused at her defense of her violin.

Obviously once away from the music world she was used to, she shouldn't expect the same reverence she received in New York.

That's what she wanted, more anonymity and less pressure. She couldn't have it both ways.

In only a few moments, Kirk suggested they leave. Angelica could see Webb Francis was growing tired. Would he truly be up to returning home in a few days? She hoped so, but doubts began to grow.

As they walked out of the hospital, several people greeted Kirk—mostly women, Angelica noticed. Not that she blamed them. He looked even better today than when she'd first met him. The jeans were newer and fit like a glove. The shirt with the sleeves rolled back wasn't as fitted as the T-shirt had been, but still showed off the perfect physique. His dark eyes seemed to notice everything, and the smile he gave when greeting people sent her heat index spiking.

"Need anything here before we return to Smoky Hollow?" he asked when they approached the motorcycle.

"How would I carry it if I did?" she asked.

"We'd manage."

He was looking at her with the same intensity. Those dark eyes seem to see right down into her soul.

She felt light-headed. Looking at the motorcycle, she drew in a breath.

"I'll wait until I get to Smoky Hollow. If I'm really going to stay in Webb Francis's house, I'll need some food and things. The store there sells everything I'd need, right?"

"Pretty much. We'll stop for lunch before heading home. All right with you?"

She nodded, interested in what she would see of Bryceville. A larger town than Smoky Hollow, it was nothing like New York. But few places were.

By the time they reached Smoky Hollow in the mid afternoon, Angelica's head was swimming with new impressions and ideas. She had not, however, learned much about her guide.

He'd driven through Bryceville pointing out landmarks. They'd eaten at a little café on a side street where everyone seemed to know Kirk and were friendly and welcoming when introduced to her.

The ride back had been hot, the heat couldn't be outrun and she was feeling limp when they stopped in front of the store.

"Stock up on what you need. I'll be back and we'll get your things from Sally Ann's, then I'll take you to Webb Francis's place," he said when she got off the bike.

Handing him her helmet, she eyed the bike. "On that?"

"I have a truck."

She wondered why they hadn't taken the truck into Bryceville. But she merely nodded.

"Thank you, I appreciate that. This is such a small town, once I'm settled, I'm sure I can walk everywhere."

"Pretty much."

He pushed back, then took off.

The two permanent fixtures on the porch asked her how she'd liked Bryceville.

"Very nice," she replied as she passed to enter the store.

She'd heard people in small towns knew everybody's business. What a novelty that was. She didn't know all the neighbors in her apartment floor and she'd lived there three years.

Stepping inside, Angelica was immediately fascinated by the old building. The wooden floors beneath her feet were worn, as if from a hundred years of shoppers. The shelves were not as tall as in most supermarkets, but from the assortment of merchandise, she realized the store carried all she'd need—just not in the vast quantities of larger establishments.

Bella Smith was the shopkeeper and as friendly as Angelica was coming to expect. The woman had her confiding her plans to move to Webb Francis's home and the fact Kirk was helping before the shopping cart was half filled.

"He helps everyone. Such a contrast to his grandfather," the woman said, watching as Angelica added pasta to her shopping cart.

"His grandfather lives around here?" Angelica asked, curious about her reluctant guide.

Could she get the shopkeeper to tell if Kirk was married or not?

"Sure does. Lives down on Doe Lane. Mean old man. He raised Kirk. Amazing to me the boy turned out as well as he did."

Angelica blinked at the older woman's choice of words. Boy? The man was all man and then some.

When she had enough food to last a few days, she went to the checkout counter.

"How's Webb Francis doing?" Bella asked as she rang up the purchases.

"Seemed very weak and tired to me. But he's hoping to come back home before long."

"Good thing Kirk checks in on him. It could have been a lot worse if Kirk hadn't found him when he did. There, I think that's all you wanted. You let me know if you need anything else."

"Thank you."

Angelica looked at the four bags of groceries, wondering how she was going to get them to Webb Francis's home. She'd stocked up so she didn't need to shop again soon, but now she wondered if she would have been better off with just a few things to tide her over until morning.

"Ready?"

Kirk walked in the store. His timing was perfect.

She nodded, careful to take a deep breath in case she didn't get to breathe again until she got used to him being around. Was there something in the air that was making her crazy around this man? She wasn't even sure she liked him. He didn't seem to like her that much either.

"Got your truck?" Bella asked.

"Sure, lots to carry," he said, taking two of the bags as if they weighed nothing. Angelica picked up the third and Bella the last one. When she stepped out on the porch, Angelica saw a big pickup truck parked nose in. Kirk placed the bags in the area behind the passenger seat of the extended cab. He quickly took hers and Bella's and stowed them as well.

"Let's go," he said, pushing back the passenger seat so Angelica could climb in.

"If you have this, why did we take the motorcycle this morning?" she asked when he climbed in behind the wheel and started the engine. Refreshing cool air blew from the vents. She relished the coolness, moving one vent so the air blew directly on her face.

"This is practical. The bike is fun."

Angelica thought about that. When was the last time she'd done something for pure fun?

She needed to get a life. She loved music, but felt very one-dimensional with all the focus on the classical and modern compositions and the endless hours of practice.

So now she was expanding music to include other aspects. What else could she expand in her life?

She glanced at Kirk, considering. She didn't have a steady man in her life. And up until now, that hadn't bothered her. She still didn't know if he was married, but there was no ring on his left hand.

They made quick work of getting her few possessions from Sally Ann's and then headed back past the store and on down a quiet street heading east.

"How far from town is Webb Francis's house?" she asked when they were underway.

Kirk didn't answer. She glanced at him. He was watching the road. Catching a glimpse of her movement, he flicked a look her way.

"How far is it from town?" she repeated, louder. The motor wasn't that loud. Was he preoccupied?

"How far? How about here?" He pulled into a graveled driveway. Twenty feet in front of her sat a charming little cottage. White with bright blue trim, it looked like a doll's house. The front yard consisted of a lawn in need of mowing, one rosebush bent over with blossoms and lots of shade trees. It was a spacious lot. The only neighbor she could see was the log cabin to the right.

"Easy walk to town," she said.

"Get settled in and I'll take you around and introduce you. Then you're on your own."

"You don't have to do that," she said stiffly.

It sounded like he wanted no more to do with her than she wanted with him. But as a favor to his friend he'd follow through. he could relieve him of that obligation. She'd do fine on her own.

"Webb Francis asked me to."

He got out and slung her backpack over one shoulder. She jumped out and retrieved her violin case before he could touch it. Taking one of the bags of groceries, she stepped to the front door and waited. Kirk came a minute later carrying two more bags.

"Open it, it's not locked."

Angelica blinked. She tried the door. It wasn't locked.

"Amazing."

She stepped into a comfortable living room. Through the opening in the back wall she glimpsed the kitchen.

"Come on, through here," he said, passing her and heading straight to the kitchen.

She liked the spaciousness of what she saw. From the outside the cottage looked tiny. But it was easily three times the size of her apartment.

She put her bag of groceries on the old farmhouse-style table and looked around. Kirk headed back to the truck for the last of the groceries. The appliances weren't new, but looked well kept.

The window in the back gave a view of more woods, the thick green foliage shading the backyard. She pushed it open and let the warm air in. The house smelled a bit musty. She didn't mind the heat, savoring the different scents that were so unfamiliar.

He dropped the bag on the table.

"Guest bedrooms are off the hall to the right when you entered. Bath farther along. Might need sheets which are probably in the hall linen closet. Webb Francis's room is in the back. Need anything else?"

"No, I'm fine. Thank you."

"Do you want to go to town today or wait until the morning?" he asked, his dark eyes gazing into hers. His entire body seemed focused on her.

"Tomorrow's fine. I'll settle in this afternoon."

She wanted to look away, but those dark eyes held. What was Kirk thinking as he gazed at her? She never could figure out how other people thought. She held her breath until he nodded and turned.

He glanced around.

"If you need anything, holler. I'm next door."

"Next door?" she repeated.

He had the log house she'd seen when they arrived.

"Problem with that?"

She shook her head quickly. The last thing she wanted was for Kirk Devon to have a clue how badly he affected her equilibrium.

"Tomorrow at ten then."

Angelica followed him to the door and watched as he backed the truck out of the driveway and in only seconds pulled into the one by the log house. He parked the truck on the far side. Behind was another building. Was that his garage? It was hard to see through the thick growth of trees and shrubs. There was so much green.

Sighing softly, she returned to the kitchen to put the food away. Then she wandered around the cottage, checking each room. She ended up in the small room Webb Francis had told her about. It was lined with shelves that seemed to hold an inordinate amount of sheet music. There were harmonicas in cases on one shelf, two violins, a banjo and a mountain dulcimer. Two music stands stood in the corner, two folding chairs leaned against one wall. She ran her fingertips over the strings of the dulcimer. She'd only heard one played once.

She leafed through some of the sheet music. She recognized a couple of songs from the class at the conservatory. For the first time in a long while she felt some excitement about playing.

It was growing dark when Angelica put her violin down. She hadn't played like that in a long time. Feeling lighter and happy for the first time in months, she went to prepare her dinner. It was after nine. She'd eat, go to bed and be up in the morning in time to go with Kirk to meet people Webb Francis thought could help her.

Getting ready for bed a little later, she glanced out the bedroom window toward Kirk's house. It was dark. But the building behind was lighted. What was he doing in the garage this late at night? Tinkering with his car?

She stared at the building for a long time, lost in thought about her reluctant neighbor and the wild fantasies she was weaving in her imagination. He'd probably laugh himself silly if he knew. She sighed softly and turned away. She was here to get rejuvenated, not fall for some man who lived hundreds of miles from New York City.

Chapter Three

It was early when Kirk kick-started his bike and headed for his grandfather's place. He checked on the old man two or three times a week. Pops rarely came to town any more—preferring his own company on the farm to mingling with others. No one cared. He had the disposition of a surly bear.

But he was the one who raised Kirk and he had a deep abiding affection for the old man.

When he pulled into the yard a short time later, the old hound barked and ran to greet him. Soon Pops came out of the back.

"You here for breakfast?" he asked gruffly.

"If there's any going, I am," Kirk said.

He took off his helmet and propped up the motorcycle. Glancing around he saw a farm still going strong. He hoped he had the energy and determination when he was in his seventies that his grandfather did.

"How're you doing for eggs?" Kirk asked as he drew closer.

There were no hugs. They didn't even shake hands. But Kirk felt the love for the old man as an integral part of himself.

"Sent some over to Bella yesterday. Plenty laying now. Come on in. Coffee's on and you can cook the biscuits."

The two prepared their breakfast as they had many mornings when Kirk was growing up. His mother had abandoned them when he'd been about two. He really had no memory of her. His grandmother had long ago left the grouchy old man. After his father's death, it had been Kirk and Pops.

"Saw Webb Francis yesterday," Kirk said after he put the biscuits in the oven to cook.

"Is he getting better?" his grandfather asked.

"Appears to be, though he looks like death warmed over. Says he'll be home soon, but I don't think so."

"You keeping an eye on his place?"

His grandfather might not be the most personable of men, but he had a strong sense of duty he'd instilled in Kirk.

"I am. He's got someone staying there a few days. A woman from New York."

"What's she doing here?"

"Came to learn some folk songs from Webb Francis."

He looked at his grandson sharply. "Pretty, that woman?"

"Too thin. Has tired eyes. Seems to switch from being all haughty to scared of her own shadow and back again."

"She won't stay long."

"They never do, do they?" Kirk said, thinking about his family's history with women.

"Best thing I can say of my marriage was your father. His best was you."

Kirk nodded. He didn't have a marriage to boast of.

Would he ever find someone to make a family with? He'd once thought he and Alice would marry. But she upped and went off to Atlanta and found a rich attorney.

Once he'd had his fill of seeing the world, he'd wanted to settle in Smoky Hollow. How different life would have been with a few changes along the way.

"You should marry, have some kids. I wouldn't mind having a great-grandchild," Pops said gruffly.

Kirk was surprised to hear him say that. "Thought you believe men are better off without women."

"Can't make a baby alone," Pops said.

For a second, Kirk thought of the pretty woman from New York. It'd been a while since anyone had caught his attention. She appeared too uptight to want children was his instant assessment. But for a moment, he wondered what it would be like to kiss her, to see her eyes blaze with awareness and desire. Was she cool as her coloring or could she flare into passion with the right man?

Stupid thought, as if he could ever be the right man. Alice had been from Smoky Hollow and had moved away as soon as she was able. No city slicker would hang around beyond the summer. And he wasn't interested in moving to New York.

"Have to make do with me," he said.

His grandfather shrugged.

"Works for me."

After eating a hearty breakfast, he helped his grandfather with chores. The man wasn't slowing down much, but he was in his seventies. Maybe Kirk should suggest he get some help, hire a man to work alongside him.

Farming wasn't for Kirk. He didn't mind helping out from time to time, but he and Pops had settled a long time ago that Kirk wasn't going to take on the family farm. He liked building and carving. Lately the building side had slowed, giving him more time for the carving.

"Might go over to Bryceville later this week, check in on Webb Francis," Pops said later when Kirk was getting ready to leave to meet Angelica.

"He'd like that. Tell him I'm introducing his friend around."

Pops looked at Kirk.

"Bring her by here one day."

Kirk shook his head. "You come to town. You haven't been in weeks. Do you good."

"I'm busy."

Kirk laughed. "Take it easy, Pops. I'll come by in a day or two."

He drove the short distance home and left the bike while he walked to his next-door neighbor's house.

Knocking on the front door, he was surprised to see Angelica open it instantly, almost as if she'd been standing behind it waiting for him. A check of his watch showed it wasn't quite ten, so he wasn't late. She stepped onto the porch, closing the door behind her. He caught a whiff of some light floral scent, blending with that of grass and the roses running riot in Webb Francis's yard.

Her hair was sleek and glowing in the sunlight. Tied back he couldn't get a good estimate of if it was wavy or not. But that honey color was delicious. Her eyes were staring at him as he caught her gaze.

"What?"

"Are we going? Or are we just standing here for the rest of the morning."

He started to agree with standing and staring at her. She was pretty as a spring morning.

And totally off limits if her attitude was anything to go by.

"We're going. Got everything you need?"

She lifted her tote a few inches, then turned and stepped off the porch.

Walking beside her he registered the state of the lawn. He'd have to get over and cut the grass before they had to get a harvester in.

She said something. He looked at her.

"Say again?"

"What?"

"What you said, can you repeat it?"

"I asked how long it's going to take to get to wherever we are going and why aren't we driving?"

"I thought New Yorkers walked everywhere," he said, ignoring the first part of the comment.

"I usually take cabs."

"Lazy," he teased.

She flared up, then caught the gleam in his eye and relaxed a fraction, giving a rueful smile.

"Maybe a bit. But I don't want to be walking down a busy street with my violin. It could get damaged."

"You don't take it everywhere."

She nodded. "Pretty much."

"So are you famous or something?"

She shook her head.

"Why would you think that?"

"Webb Francis seemed impressed—said he could learn something from you and he's the best fiddle player around."

"Violin," she murmured.

"Say again?"

She stopped and faced him straight on. "Violin," she said loud and clear.

"I'm deaf in one ear, have a hearing loss in the other," he said.

Her eyes widened.

"I didn't know. Sorry."

She was almost yelling.

He leaned closer, taking in that light floral scent, and the heat of her.

"I can hear normal tones for the most part if I'm facing the person talking. Don't yell."

Her eyes gazed into his and he felt a tightening in his gut. The blue was flawless, like the deep summer blue of the skies over Kentucky. She didn't look away and he felt as if she was drawing him in closer, until he could almost brush his lips across hers, taste the sweetness he knew he'd find, discover if passion lurked beneath the cool exterior.

She blinked and stepped back.

"Where are we going?" she asked.

"First to the library. Mary Margaret McBride has video tapes of other music festivals and CDs. Get to know her and you can watch and listen to them to see who you want to talk to. Then if I can find them, I'll introduce you to Dottie and Paul, two of the members in the group Webb Francis plays with. We'll run into Gina one of these days. She's coordinating the festival—doing it all now that Webb Francis is out of commission."

The day was growing warm, but Angelica didn't notice as much as she had the previous day. Kirk's stride was longer than hers so she had to walk briskly to keep up. She hadn't really thought he was deaf—or partly deaf—when she'd shown her annoyance by stopping in the street.

How had it happened? Had he been born deaf? Maybe that explained the intense way he focused on people when they spoke—to better understand what they were saying. Did he read lips?

She searched her mind for what little she knew about deafness. Sometimes people could hear certain ranges of sound. With his remaining hearing, did he have full range or limited? She didn't feel she knew him well enough to ask, but she was curious.

She couldn't imagine not hearing. Listening to music, hearing the birds chirping, talking with friends—how much she'd miss if she were deaf.

"Do you work?" she asked as they turned a corner. Ten feet ahead was the start of a sidewalk. They had arrived in the town proper.

"Sure."

"You haven't for the last three days."

"Neither have you," he replied.

"Are you on vacation, too?"

"Is this your vacation?"

She bit her lip and studied the buildings and storefronts as they walked by.

"Sort of."

She wasn't going to explain. She wasn't sure she could. The drudgery of constant practice and rehearsals, the limited social outlets, the pressure from her parents to achieve more and more had finally reached the point where she wasn't sure about anything any more.

Music had once enchanted her. Now it was a chore. Her escape was an attempt to find the joy in music again. Try something else. Find herself. She couldn't envision herself playing the violin to the exclusion of everything else for the next fifty years.

Should she try another instrument? Think about another career? She was too burned out to do any of that.

The town consisted of two main streets, intersected by cross streets for five blocks. The predominant vehicles parked at the curb were dusty pickup trucks. Except for a couple of men talking in front of the bank, and a woman farther down the block gazing into one of the windows, the place seemed deserted. She really had arrived at another world.

"Where are all the people?" she asked.

"Mostly at work, I expect."

She glanced at him again.

"What do you do for a living?"

"Construction. A little whittling. Whatever comes along. Library's right here."

He held open one of the double doors leading into a single story frame building. The sign hanging from the overhanging roof simply said Library.

It was blessedly cool inside. Angelica's spirits rose.

A round woman with a merry smile looked up from the front desk.

"Good morning," she sang out.

Angelica smiled involuntarily. The woman's happiness was almost contagious.

"Mary Margaret, I'd like you to meet Angelica Cannon. She's staying at Webb Francis's while he's in hospital. She plays the fiddle and wants to study some of the music played around here."

"Welcome to Smoky Hollow. How's Webb Francis doing?" she asked, looking first at Angelica and then Kirk.

"Mending. Angelica's from New York. Plays some."

"I heard you have tapes of some of the music gatherings here. I'd like to listen to them some time," Angelica expanded.

"We've got a fine media room, with a DVD player and CD players. Plus a VCR for old recordings. And a subscription to streaming events. Or you can check them out and take the CDs home with you. I know Webb Francis has a player."

"I'm just visiting."

"Well, with Webb Francis and Kirk vouching for you, I reckon you can get a temporary library card. Want to look now?"

"We'll stop back by on the way home. Pick her out a couple if you would, Mary Margaret. She wants to hear mountain music."

Mary Margaret laughed. "Well, she came to the right place for that. Come on in any time. I'm here most days."

Angelica agreed and turned to follow Kirk when he headed out.

"No regular hours?" she asked once the door closed behind them.

"She's here most of the time. If she's not, folks just go in and help themselves, leaving her a note on which books they borrowed."

Angelica didn't use the public library much in New York, but she couldn't imagine it operating the same way.

Kirk turned down one of the side streets and walked swiftly.

"Are we in a hurry?" she asked, catching her breath as she tried to keep up.

He stopped and looked at her.

"I want to show you around like Webb Francis asked. Then you're on your own."

"I can manage now. I'll talk with the librarian and get her recommendations. You're off the hook."

He looked up at the canopy of trees overhead, then down the road.

"Not yet. I said I'd take you around and I will."

"I absolve you of all obligations. Face it, it's a chore and I don't want to be a burden."

"I said I'd do it."

She didn't move when he stepped forward. Turning, he waited.

"I can start at the library. Listen to the CDs. Talk to Mary Margaret and find out more about the festival, where to find music, what to look for. I don't need a guide. For heaven's sake, I've toured Europe."

Not that it meant much. She'd visited London, Paris and Moscow and never saw much except what was between the hotel and concert hall. She'd never visited her own nation's capital, much less seen more of the USA.

Primitive, that's what she thought when she thought of Appalachia. A land where people kept to old ways and poverty had a stronghold. She hadn't realized how pretty it was. Or how much she'd like the people she'd meet. They were genuine and honest, and friendly as could be.

"Come on, I don't have all day," he said, reaching out to take her arm.

She felt the touch like a live wire and jerked away. Feeling stupid with her reaction, she tried to cover it.

"It's hot like you said. I hadn't expected it to be this warm."

What startled her was her own reaction. Taking a deep breath she tried to quell her roiling senses. She'd been touched before. She'd had her share of crushes while growing up. She was a grown woman, not to be flustered by an impersonal touch, no matter how dynamic the man was. She refused to start believing he was special. He was her reluctant guide, nothing more.

Yet he continued to stare at her, as if waiting for more words. Heat washed through her at the intensity. She wanted to forget about the music, sit down with him and learn all she could about Kirk Devon.

She had to stop thinking like that. It was her own convoluted thought process had her confused. She wasn't looking for complications—but simplicity. She wanted to study a different kind of music, see if she could recover her passion for playing.

Or discover something else that would bring joy to her life. Not get hot and bothered watching a sexy Kentucky man who could barely stand to be around her.

Stalemate. They stared at each other, neither moving.

She didn't know why she found him so appealing. He wore

jeans, worn and faded after years of wear. His blue chambray shirt was opened at the throat with its sleeves rolled back. He looked totally different from the successful businessmen she was used to. He probably didn't even own a suit. He was in his element, she was the fish out of water, yet something attracted her. The awareness of him grew each time they were together. She wanted to touch that throat, feel the heat of his skin against hers. Hear him laugh, learn what he liked and disliked.

"Coming or not?" he finally asked.

"I guess. But you don't have to go out of your way to introduce me around. I can manage."

"Be easier in a small town to have someone vouch for you."

"Networking."

She nodded.

He laughed.

"Big city girl."

He turned and walked away. After a moment, Angelica hurried to catch up.

The sooner she got this over, the sooner she'd be on her own.

It was after lunch when Kirk walked with Angelica back to the cottage. She'd met a half dozen people, including Dottie Ferguson and Paul Cantwell who played with Webb Francis. Each person she met had been friendly and happy to talk with her about the songs she wanted to learn. She had collected phone numbers and jotted down names and addresses and drawn a sketchy map so she could find her way around Smoky Hollow.

Kirk was hard to figure out, she mused as he stopped in the road in front of her house. He'd done his duty, actually gone beyond in her opinion, buying her lunch at the local diner. Now he was free of any obligation. She should be relieved. She felt cut adrift.

He reached out and took the small spiral bound notebook she still carried in her hand and wrote his phone number down.

"You're right next door, but it is easier to call sometimes. Let me know if you need anything."

"I can manage."

His intense gaze was something she wished she could get used to. She wasn't accustomed to people focusing so intensely on her and it caused a chain reaction inside that threatened her equilibrium. His gaze dropped to her mouth. She wasn't talking.

Was he thinking what she suddenly thought about? Kisses, long and drugging and fantastic.

She groaned softly and looked away before she did something beyond foolish.

"Thank you."

Hurrying toward the cottage she resisted the urge to look behind her, to watch as he walked away. Once inside, she leaned against the front door, refusing to look though every cell in her body clamored to do just that.

Pushing away, she went into the kitchen. She'd have something cold to drink then decide what to do next.

Resisting temptation proved too much. She looked out the side window of the kitchen. She saw nothing but the house next door. He either had already gone inside, or had gone somewhere else.

Soon thereafter Angelica retraced her steps to the library. Mary Margaret sat with a large pile of books in front of her, jotting notes on a tablet. She looked up and smiled when Angelica entered.

"Come to hear those CDs?" she asked.

"If now is a good time."

"Of course. Come back to the media center. They're readily

available. I'll show you the lot and then you choose and play whichever ones you want. Take some home if you like. The DVDs are clearly labeled, too."

Angelica dutifully followed. The room in the back was bright and airy with an expanse of windows across the back wall. Several new computers lined a side wall, none in use at the moment. There was a large-screen TV with audio-video equipment beside it, a DVD player, a VCR, and several other items she didn't know. Two CD players with headphones were on a table by themselves. Across the middle of the room was a chest-high double row of shelves housing CDs. How did such a small town get such a state-of-the-art media room in their library?

As if she'd asked the question aloud, Mary Margaret smiled at her and said, "Kirk gave us all this, isn't it grand? I have one of the best media rooms in the state, thanks to his donations. Makes some of my colleagues in other towns envious, I can tell you. Come here and I'll explain the system."

She led Angelica to the shelves and explained how the music CDs were sorted.

Once she was sure Angelica understood how to operate the equipment, she left her on her own. Angelica picked out a CD that had Webb Francis's name on it. The earphones were excellent. How had. Kirk managed to sponsor all this? Construction must pay more than she thought.

In no time she was enjoying the music. From one fast paced song, to a very slow ballad, to music that sounded like someone could dance a jig to it, the recording played tunes so foreign to her ear she couldn't believe it had existed all this time and she'd only touched a bit of it in her one class at the conservatory.

By the end of the CD, she could hear more and more people from the town joining in. It sounded as if Webb Francis had just recorded a jam session that grew and grew and then burned it on a CD.

Soon the background changed again. Now it sounded as if they were playing for an audience. Casual, informal, with clapping at the end of each song. She heard people calling requests. It was as far from a symphony hall as anything could be.

As was the music. The fast songs were upbeat and fun. The ballads tragic and sad. The wide range had her interested as she hadn't been in a long time.

"I have to run out to do a couple of errands," Mary Margaret said from the door to the media room.

Angelica pulled off the headphones. "I'll be ready to go in a minute."

"No, no, dear, you stay as long as you want. If you leave before I return, just make sure the door shuts behind you. It's windy outside. Wouldn't be surprised if we have some rain. Finding what you want?"

"I am, even more than what I expected," Angelica said with a smile.

She resumed listening, jotting notes of songs she wanted to hear more of. And wondering who could identify the songs where they didn't announce them before they began to play. From the enthusiastic response to many, they were familiar favorites.

Kirk knocked on the door at Webb Francis's house. He waited, scanning the trees that were already swaying in the strong breeze pushing in a storm. Angelica didn't answer. He tried again. No one home. Where would she have gone? To the library, he bet.

Sometimes the thunderstorms knocked out power. When he realized a storm was brewing, he thought he better show her where candles were and how to use the generator for the water pump.

Now he thought he'd better find her in case it began to rain before she came home. He didn't really want to be walking around in a thunderstorm, nor should she. He drove the truck for the short distance to town.

When he stepped up on the porch of the library, even he could hear the trees rustling in the growing wind. He felt the strong breeze across his face. The dark clouds from the west seemed to build above him as he detected a hint of a rain in the air. He bet Angelica had no idea how quickly storms could brew in the mountains.

Stepping inside, he saw the main room of the library was empty. The lights were on in the media room, so he headed back there. The sudden drumming on the roof signaled the arrival of the rain. It sounded like a gully washer.

Angelica looked up when he stepped in the room.

"What're you doing here?" she asked.

The rumble of thunder answered her.

"Stopped by the house to let you know about candles. The storms around here can knock out power for hours or even days at a time. Now it's pouring," he said. "You'll need a ride home."

He walked to the bank of windows and looked out. Already a torrential downpour began making mud. The rain came so hard it bounced on the ground. The noise on the metal roof sounded like drums.

Angelica came to stand beside him, staring in dismay at the rain.

"If we go out in that, we'll be soaked within seconds."

"I brought my truck. We'll make a run for it," he offered.

"The librarian went out on errands. She said to close up if I left before she returned."

A white bolt of lightning lit the sky, the crash of thunder

almost immediate. Angelica jumped and bumped against Kirk. He reached out to steady her at the same time the power went out. Only the dim light from outside illuminated the room. With the dark clouds overhead the day was as dark as twilight.

"My guess is she'll stay where she is until the storm passes," he said.

"Shouldn't we stay here?"

"It could last for a while. Now that the power's out, what will you do?"

He was right. With no power, she couldn't listen to the CDs. Might as well go back home.

When they arrived at Webb Francis's place, Kirk parked right next to the front porch, passenger side closest. Angelica dashed to the porch, getting wet. She shook her head when she was sheltered and watched as Kirk raced up, taking the three steps in one leap.

"Come on, I'll show you where the candles are and a flashlight."

He led the way into the kitchen, reached into the cupboard over the refrigerator and pulled down a handful of candles and a huge flashlight. He pulled matches from a drawer and lined them all up on the counter in front of a window.

"You'll have some daylight until evening. Then it'll really get dark."

"Thank you."

She tried to remember the last time they'd lost power in New York. She didn't think they ever had since she lived there.

"What do you do for dinner?" she asked.

"I have a gas range, cook on that."

He glanced at Webb Francis's electric stove.

"You're welcome to come over for dinner."

She hesitated. She had to eat.

"If the power isn't back on I'll come over later."

She escorted him to the porch. The rain seemed to be coming down in sheets, blowing in under the overhang on the side as the wind drove it.

"Call if you need anything."

He stood so close he was crowding her against the porch railing, invading her space. She could smell the hint of aftershave even so late in the day. Her heart began drumming as if her body recognized his. Which was dumb, she'd barely touched the man. Yet something primal seemed to shimmer between them.

He was so close she could feel his breath on her face. She looked up and saw the intensity in his eyes.

"If I need anything, which I doubt, I'll call."

She wanted to reach out and touch him. Her fingers actually yearned to feel those hard arms, the power of his muscles beneath them.

He held his position for a moment longer and she wondered if he could read her mind. When he stepped back and turned as if to leave, she almost grabbed the railing so her wobbly knees wouldn't give way. A whirlwind couldn't shake her any more than being close to Kirk did.

She drew in a deep breath. Something was moving in the road. Frowning, she peered out into the rain.

"Is someone walking in this downpour?" she asked.

Kirk paused at the edge of the porch and looked. He lifted his hand in a short wave.

A moment later a young boy ran across the yard and up to the porch.

"Is Webb Francis back?" he asked.

He carried an umbrella, but it hadn't kept him dry in the blowing rain. His jeans were wet, his hair was tousled. He looked to be about eight years old.

"No, he's in hospital in Bryceville," Kirk said, stooping down to face the boy at eye level.

Angelica wondered if that helped him hear.

The boy's face dropped.

"He's giving me fiddle lessons. I haven't had one all week. And I need to practice so I can be in the festival."

The sad look on his face touched Angelica.

Kirk looked up at her.

"You're in luck, Sam, this lady plays the fiddle. She can teach you until Webb Francis gets home."

Chapter Four

"I can't teach him how to play," Angelica protested. She'd never taught anyone how to play anything.

"Make sure he know the basics, let him practice. Webb Francis will be home in a few days. He'll probably manage sitting in a chair while Sam plays. How hard can it be?"

"I don't know anything about children," she countered, looking at the little boy.

He was so small she wondered how he'd hold a violin.

Then she thought about when she'd been his age—maybe even younger. She'd been so thrilled to learn to play—back in the day when all things were fantastic and the reality of constant practice hadn't dimmed her enthusiasm. She'd been able to make music.

The echo of that thrill seemed dim in all that had transpired over the decades since.

"Sam Tanner, meet Angelica Cannon. She plays the fiddle and can help you along until Webb Francis comes home."

Kirk made the announcement as if she'd agreed.

"Hi," the boy said with a hopeful gleam in his eyes. "Can you teach me?"

"Make me out to be the bad guy if I say no," she muttered.

"Say again?" Kirk said standing and watching her with amusement in his gaze.

He knew what he'd done. How could she disappoint a child?

"Never mind. I guess we can give it a try." She didn't sound very enthusiastic, because she had no clue where to begin.

"Thanks, Ms. Cannon. I have to use Webb Francis's fiddle, I don't have one of my own. But he lets me."

"Maybe Angelica could let you try hers," Kirk said.

"No way. That instrument is worth thousands. If Webb Francis said the boy could use one of his, then he needs to use that one."

"His name is Sam."

"Sam," Angelica repeated offering a smile to the child.

She wasn't used to being around children. Her life had been devoted to the violin since she was six.

"Come on inside, then, and we'll see. You coming?" she asked Kirk when Sam began walking to the front door.

"Naw, I've got things to do. Besides, I can't hear enough to really enjoy the music."

She almost laughed. How much enjoyment would there be with a beginning child? Then the reality of what he said hit. It made her sad to think he couldn't enjoy all the sounds of the world. She was a little burned out, but she could never imagine life without music.

"If the power's off still at dinner, come and eat with me."

He said goodbye to Sam and admonished him to be good, then dashed back to the truck and backed out of the short driveway.

Once inside, doubts assailed. She truly didn't know how to teach.

Sam seemed to know exactly what to do, however. He stowed his umbrella in a stand near the front door and walked confidently into the music room. He picked up one of the violins and turned to her, his eyes shining.

"Show me what you already know," she said.

He spent a few minutes playing the strings. It sounded in good tune which surprised her. The damp humid air had to have some effect on the instrument. He tightened one string, tried again and then smiled. The next thing she knew he was playing an unfamiliar song, slowly and hesitantly, but she could recognize a definite melody.

When he was finished, he lowered his arms and looked hopeful.

"What was that song?" she asked, sitting in a nearby chair.

"'Granny Does Your Dog Bite.' It's the one I want to play in the festival. Webb Francis was helping me learn it. It's supposed to go fast."

"Do you have music?" she asked.

He shook his head. "No, Webb Francis says the real artiste plays by knowing how it's suppose to sound. Do you think I can be a real artiste one day? I can practice every day if you're here."

Angelica was enchanted with the child's determination. She wasn't sure how the song should sound, but if he was happy with it, she'd go along with that.

"Yes, I think you'll do great at the music festival."

She studied the little boy for a moment, then jumped up.

"I'll get my violin and we'll have a session together, how's that?"

"Violin?" he asked.

"My fiddle," she said, giving in.

When in Kentucky…

Hurrying to her room, she retrieved the old instrument and almost laughed aloud. What would her parents think if they knew she wanted to play American folk music on the priceless heirloom?

Kirk stoked the fire and sat back. It was growing dark. The brunt of the storm had passed by several hours ago, but the steady rain lingered. Power was still out. Probably would be until morning. The air had grown cooler. He'd made a small fire in the fireplace. Suitable for cooking hot dogs and marshmallows.

A couple of times during the afternoon, he'd glanced over at the house next door. He hadn't seen Sam leave. Nor had he seen any activity over there. What was Angelica doing to while away the afternoon?

He was about to go over to make sure she was okay when he heard a knock on the door. Opening it a moment later he saw his neighbor. Droplets of rain shone on her hair. She wore a sweatshirt that was already damp on the shoulders.

"You should have a hammer by the door, I almost broke my hand banging," she grumbled as she stared up at him.

"Most friends just come in and let me know they're here."

"I'm not a friend. I don't know the mores of this area. In New York, one most definitely knocks first."

And waits while the other person unlocked several locks.

He nodded.

"Come for dinner?"

He stepped back and gestured her in.

She looked around the living room, her eyes widening in surprise. Kirk knew she expected rustic to go with the exterior of the log home, but the inside was comfortable and quite modern. The comfy sofa was long enough he could lie down if watching TV, or wanting a nap. The matching arm chairs were sturdy enough for any of his wild friends, and the colors were ones Alice had talked about before she walked out. He knew enough to use them to make his home comfortable. It was his place, now, and he no longer thought about her every time he walked into the room.

"This is lovely," Angelica said.

"About ready for dinner. Come on through to the kitchen. We'll use the fire for our meal, but you can help carry things out. Want to take off your wet sweatshirt?"

She nodded, and he hung it over the back of a chair. It should dry before long, it wasn't that wet.

She dutifully followed him into the kitchen, exclaiming in delight when she saw it. It was less than five years old and he'd spared no expense when building. He wanted something that would last.

"Beautiful. Do you cook all the time?" she asked, turning around to see everything.

"I cook my own meals."

"Gourmet cooking?"

She brushed her fingertips across the edge of the stainless steel gas range.

"Hardly. Hamburgers, hot dogs, steaks, pretty limited repertoire."

Probably seemed boring to someone from New York.

He pulled hot dogs and buns and condiments from the refrigerator and piled them on the counter. Angelica picked up some and carried them into the living room. In only a few moments all the items they needed for dinner were on the small table near the fire.

He pulled out two sticks he'd cut from a willow earlier and handed her one.

She stared at it.

"What is this for?"

"Thread on your hot dog like this," he said, taking one and poking the stick in lengthwise. "Then we hold it over the fire to cook."

"You're kidding."

She watched a moment then with an air of determination followed suit and soon had her own hot dog cooking over the flames.

"When they're done, we'll pull them off in the bun, top with condiments and have a feast," he said, suiting actions to words.

Munching on the hot dog a few minutes later, Kirk watched Angelica eat. She was dainty, testing each mouthful as if uncertain.

"Don't like hot dogs?"

"I don't eat them much," she said, taking another bite. She nodded. "These are good."

Kirk couldn't remember having someone over to camp out while the power was gone. Usually he would either eat alone, or head out to the café which had a generator for situations like this.

"This is fun," she said with a hint of surprise.

"Tell me how the lesson went."

She nodded, still chewing. Then she swallowed and smiled.

"He's surprisingly good. It's not what I would have started him on, but I guess Webb Francis thought he could do it. I think I learned more than he did. Practice might have him ready for the festival. I followed him, let the music take hold and was able to play along. Just what I came down here for. I didn't know my first foray would be with a little boy. We played Granny Does Your Dog Bite, know it?"

"Of course."

He moved back and leaned against the front of the sofa, stretching his feet out.

"That was nice of you, New York, to help him."

She finished her hot dog, put down the plate and scooted back to sit beside him. It was too warm to sit very close to the fire. The rain had cooled things down, but not that much.

"I liked it. Which surprised me. I'm an only child and have never been around children."

"Except when you were one," he said.

"Not much then—except in school. I had to practice in the afternoons."

"Why?"

"I was a child prodigy and my parents wanted me to make the most of my talent."

"So what was that like?"

Angelica began telling him a bit about growing up in Boston. The more Kirk heard, the more he thought of deprivation and lack. She didn't appear to have had the kind of childhood he'd enjoyed—roaming around, exploring things, hanging out with his friends. Even getting into trouble with some wild hijinks.

Instead, she painted a picture of a little girl and later a teenager who did little but study academics and the violin. She mentioned different recitals and programs she played in. Maybe if he knew more, he'd be impressed, but mostly he felt the lack.

"Doesn't that wear on you? When did you go to the beach with friends, shop at the mall, explore historic Boston?"

"No time."

She shrugged, then flicked him a quick glance before looking back at the fire.

"That's why I'm here. I want to see what else is out in the real world."

"It's still revolving around music," he commented.

His idea of seeing the world had been to actually travel—in Europe, in the U.S. and Canada. He'd worked construction once he got out of the army, wherever a job was going to earn enough money to keep traveling. Now he made an occasional trip to visit a gallery in a major city when selling a sculpture. But he liked home best.

"It's all I know. At least I'm branching out."

"What did your parents say to that?" he asked, curious about people who could put so much pressure on a child.

She stared at the fire for a long moment, then slowly said, "They don't know."

"Don't know what?"

"Where I am, what I'm doing. I'm twenty-eight years old, for heaven's sake, I don't need my parents' approval to do anything."

"No, you don't."

"I can make my own choices. And this is my choice, to learn more about folk music."

"Angel, no one's arguing with you here."

She flicked him another look.

"You're right. But this is the first time I've done anything like this. I'm shoring up my defenses," she said with a wry grin.

"Your defenses seem fine."

He reached out and took her hand. She started a moment, then relaxed. He traced the tips of her fingers.

"Do you have these insured?"

Angelica giggled. "No."

Giving in to impulse, Kirk brought her fingertips to his lips and kissed her lightly, then let go, watching as a spark flickered across her face and a blush rose in her cheeks.

Stretched out in front of the fire, he felt warm and replete. The steady drone of the rain on the roof was a pleasant background. He had better keep his distance from Angelica Cannon. Her hands had been warm and soft. Smaller than his, dainty. She intrigued him. And there was that attraction that wouldn't let go.

He was too wise in the ways of women to get hooked. She'd stay a few weeks and then be gone. Might even be a shorter visit once she realized how little there was to do in Smoky Hollow compared to New York City.

"Have you always lived here in Smoky Hollow?" she asked, mimicking him, stretching out her feet toward the fire, leaning against the sofa front.

Keeping herself busy asking him questions took her mind off the memory of his lips brushing against her fingertips.

"Did a stint in the army." He tapped his left ear. "That's how I lost hearing in this ear, mortar fire. Don't hear that much from the right either."

She wrinkled her nose.

"I can't imagine not hearing."

"I got used to it. When my tour of duty was over, I set out to see America."

"And did you?"

"Oh, yeah."

He told her about starting in New York and doing all the sights tourists did. Gradually he moved north, west, south, taking his time and going places he'd always heard about and wanted to see. Picking up construction work was easy. Working with locals helped him really know people who lived in a community. One summer he'd swung through parts of British Columbia and Alberta, dropping down to Montana and continuing his travels.

Angelica listened to Kirk and envy rose sharply within. He'd done so much in just a few years. She'd done so little. The places came alive when he told her of his exploits. Was it the tradition of the hills of Kentucky or was he a gifted storyteller? She laughed at his story of the shock of cold water when he went swimming in a lake in Yosemite. Caught her breath when he described the grandeur of the Grand Canyon. Wistfully wished she could have seen whales off the coast of British Columbia.

From time to time Kirk tossed another log on the fire, then resumed his place next to her and continued talking when she prompted with another question. Angelica knew she could listen to him all night. His deep voice resonated within her, his slow drawl had her relaxing and enjoying the evening. She had nothing else to do. It was wonderful.

"It's different for a guy. You can go wherever, work some odd jobs, move on. I only know how to play the violin," she said at one point.

"You don't strike me as the nomad type," he said.

"Who knows what type I am? I've been stuck in the same rut since I was six."

"It's past time you broke out, then."

"Yes, like to the wilds of Kentucky."

Kirk laughed.

"It's not really funny. This is quite different for me. I want to see new places, try new things. Have something different in my life. This is totally different from New York."

"Okay, maybe fate had a reason for sending you here."

He gazed at the fire for a moment. Then glanced at her.

"Until Webb Francis is up and around, I'll show you something of the wilds of Kentucky. You can learn to make a fire without matches, hike a trail, catch a fish. Bet you've never been to a county fair. We can go. And you can join in the music festival. Play something other than classical music. Really bust out."

"With my fiddle," Angelica said, feeling a sense of elation. "Would you really take me hiking and to a county fair?"

He had seemed unhappy with Webb Francis's suggestion he look out for her. Why the change of heart?

"Sure, why not?"

He reached out and took her hand. Angelica felt the jolt of

electricity, but this time she gripped his hand back, holding on and savoring the sensations. He rested the back of her hand against one thigh and smiled.

"I thought you didn't like me," she said.

He grinned.

"Jury's still out on that one, babe. Maybe I was hasty in making a judgement. Let's see what you've got going for you."

She considered what he said.

"Deal. What do you get in return?"

"A fun summer?"

"Don't you have to work?"

"I'm helping out at the Coopers' barn raising."

"It almost sounds as if you're doing the Coopers a favor helping build their barn. Are you independently wealthy?"

He grinned again, his eyes dancing. Angelica felt her heart race. The man was too potent for her. Could she really spend the summer learning more about the mountains of Kentucky and spending time with this man and not have her heart smashed to smithereens when she left?

She had no experience beyond casual flirting. Could she resist Kirk's charm, learn about the community and return to New York in September glad for the break, refreshed, and not hung up with Kirk Devon?

If she had any sense, she'd run the other way.

Yet his offer was tempting.

"Are you?" he countered.

"I have enough money saved to take time off for this."

"Don't worry, I have enough, too."

He paused, and their gazes met and held. It seemed as if he was leaning closer and closer and her heart beat frantically in her chest—

Then the lights came on in the kitchen.

"Power's back," he said, leaning backwards and glancing over at the lights.

"I should be going home. It's late."

The time had flown by. She couldn't remember when she'd enjoyed an evening so much—and all they did was talk. And hold hands. Reluctantly she slid hers from beneath his and scrambled to get up.

"I'll walk you home."

He rose easily to his feet. They stood so close she could see the fine lines around his eyes, feel the soft brush of his breath across her cheeks.

"Thank you for dinner," she said politely.

"You can repay the favor sometime," he said casually.

In only a few minutes, Angelica closed the door to the cottage and leaned against it. She'd halfway hoped he'd kiss her good night. Which was idiotic. He'd outright admitted he wasn't sure if he even liked her. Why would he want to kiss her?

She knew why she wanted to kiss him. It would be amazing. Her heart pounded just thinking about it. And her hand still held the warmth from his.

Tomorrow—she'd see him again tomorrow. Would they go hiking? She needed time to get back to the library and listen to more CDs. And Sam was coming over again in the afternoon for another practice session. Two days in town and already she had a full agenda. She grinned as she walked back to the bedroom.

It was after ten the next morning when Angelica gave up on Kirk and walked to the library. She'd risen early, eaten quickly and sat with an ear to the door expecting him to come over. He'd said he'd show her around. Yet they'd made no firm plans. Maybe he had merely been being polite.

Twice she rose and went to the window in the music room that faced Kirk's house. She saw no signs of activity. Had he gone to work on that barn? He had to work every day like most people. Smoky Hollow didn't look like it sported a lot of millionaires.

When she reached the library, Mary Margaret was sitting behind the desk and greeted her warmly.

"I thought you'd be back this morning, what with the power knocking off everything yesterday. I'm sure you didn't hear enough. Do you need any help finding anything specific?"

"I'm not really looking for anything special. I want an overview and choosing the CDs randomly seems to give me that," Angelica said.

She glanced behind her through the double doors. No sign of Kirk. She was acting like a school girl with a crush, hoping to catch a glimpse of a special guy. Raising her chin slightly, she headed back to the media room. She had better things to do than moon over some sexy man who was only showing her around because of a promise to his friend.

Two hours later, while changing one CD for another, Angelica heard Kirk's voice in the main room of the library. She took a breath, held it, trying to quell instantly clamoring nerves. Would he come back here? Was he looking for her? She strained to hear what he and Mary Margaret were saying.

She heard his footsteps. He stepped into the doorway and she looked up, immediately aware of every inch of him. His wide shoulders leaned casually against one side of the door frame. He crossed his arms over his chest and looked at her, his dark eyes focused solely on her.

"Finished?" he asked, taking note of her replacing a CD in its case.

"I've been listening for a couple of hours. I'm not finished.

It's fascinating. I love the rhythm of the songs. And the words are funny sometimes."

"Take a break. We'll go for lunch."

"I'm working with Sam this afternoon around three," she said, longing to ditch the library and go wherever he asked.

What about her vow to resist temptation?

"We'll be back by then. I picked up lunch from the store. Bella makes a great picnic basket."

"Are we taking your motorcycle?" she asked.

"Nope, walking. Come on. Best time of day."

He turned.

He seemed so sure of her, she thought, following along. She had to admit to being intrigued.

As soon as they left the library, Kirk picked up a basket sitting near the door. He nodded toward the left and they walked a short distance, then he turned and began following a well-worn path that led into the shady area of the woods that grew up right next to the town.

It felt cooler once they were sheltered from the sun. Dappled spots of sunshine moved as the leaves responded to the light breeze. It was hushed in the woods, only the sound of their footsteps and birds singing in the distance. A few puddles were visible from yesterday's storm, but the ground underfoot for the most part was packed and dry.

Angelica was enchanted. She followed, not talking. Sometimes she watched Kirk as he took long strides and seemed to be part of the nature they invaded. He was comfortable in this environment. She watched the path, lifted her gaze to the leafy roof over their heads, took a breath of the fragrant air. The trilling of the birds could almost be set to music, she thought, hurrying to keep up with him.

The path was well defined. She wouldn't get lost even if he went ahead. She wondered about the early settlers to this area. If the trees had always grown so close together, so thick, it was a wonder anyone had carved out a place in Kentucky.

When she heard the gurgling of a brook, she searched ahead of them. It had to be close. It sounded lovely. Two minutes later they stepped into a wide clearing where a rock-strewn brook roughly cut the space in half. The water splashed against and over the small stones and rocks, twisting almost back on itself once, and then headed straight down into the trees.

"This is magical," she said, taking in the pretty clearing.

Sunshine kissed the grass beneath the opening in the trees. The water gave a tireless melody. The bird song topped it off.

"Can you hear the water?"

"When I'm this close I can. I remember as a kid hearing it long before I reached the opening."

"Why aren't trees growing here?"

He put down the basket, opened it and brought out a red-and-white checked tablecloth. Shaking it out to spread on the ground, he said, "No one knows. But as long as I've been coming here it's been open like this. Almost as if there's something in the soil toxic to trees. Yet there's other vegetation growing, so it's not sterile soil."

Angelica knelt down on the edge of the cloth as he began unpacking the lunch. Cold fried chicken, buttered rolls, potato salad, and iced drinks. In no time she was enjoying the meal as much as she enjoyed the setting.

He didn't talk and neither did she. Her gaze darted around as she memorized the place. Closing her eyes once, she tried to imprint the sound of the brook and the rustle of the leaves and the bird song forever on her memory. Would she be able to recall this special moment when she was stomping through the slushy New York winters?

"Very nice," she said when she opened her eyes. Kirk leaned back on one elbow and studied the stream.

"I thought you'd like it."

"Do you come here often?"

She leaned back on one hand, staring at the brook. The water glinted in the sunshine, the pleasing sound soothing. Now that she'd eaten, she could almost take a nap.

"I haven't lately. It's not exactly a place to come alone. I eat at home."

"Thank you for bringing me, it's lovely."

"In a while, we can hike upstream a bit. About a mile farther is a waterfall which dumps into a swimming hole. We could go swimming, it's hot enough."

"I don't have a suit," she said.

"Me either, so?"

Angelica looked at him. The teasing light in his eyes gave him away. She swallowed and shook her head. He laughed.

The image of the two of them swimming without a stitch on wouldn't leave. She'd never been skinny-dipping. But she'd bet lunch that Kirk had more than once. Who with, she wondered? Girlfriends from high school? Was there a special woman in his life now? Probably not or he wouldn't be so available. Were the women in Smoky Hollow blind?

They left the picnic basket at the edge of the clearing. Kirk said it'd be safe, and there was no reason to carry it up and back.

The stream meandered. The path along its side wasn't as well defined as the one from town to the clearing had been. Sometimes they stepped over exposed roots of trees, around clumps of ferns. Once they crossed on stepping stones. Angelica wished she'd brought her phone. But it was back at the cottage turned off so her parents couldn't reach her.

She'd never expected to be hopping from rock to rock to get across some stream of water when she awoke that morning. She laughed and Kirk turned to look at her.

"This is very different from New York City," she explained.

"Better?"

She nodded, scrambling to catch up. He seemed to walk along at the same pace no matter what the terrain. She was a bit out of breath keeping up with him. And while the path was primarily in shade, it was growing warmer by the minute.

"We'll be there soon," he said, turning and heading on again.

When they reached the pool, Angelica almost suggested they follow his original idea and plunge in. She was hot and out of breath. The water looked cool and inviting. The waterfall was a three-foot-tall curtain spilling over a wide lip of rock. She'd love to swim beneath it and have it rain down on her.

"Is it deep?" she asked.

The water was so clear she could see the rocky bottom. It didn't look deep.

"About four or five feet. Very deep when one is Sam's age. Not so much now. But it's refreshing."

He stopped by the edge and trailed his hands in it. Then he flicked her with water.

Surprised, she leaned over and slapped a wave of water at him. Only a little reached her target. She danced away when he splashed her again. Laughing, she wished she could douse him.

He cupped water in his hands and started for her, devilment in his eyes. Angelica shrieked and turned to run. A second later her entire back was wet. She laughed again and turned.

"No fair, you have the advantage," she said, when he turned

to get more water. She didn't have clear access to the pond. Darting to the left, she tried to go wide, but he turned and threw water at her again.

Laughing so hard she almost fell, she reached the edge of the water. Ignoring her shoes, she waded in and began splashing water at him. He joined in and before five minutes passed they were both soaked.

Angelica plopped down at the edge of the water and just let Kirk's attack wash over her. She felt deliciously cool in the hot afternoon. She'd squish all the way home, but for now it felt marvelous.

A minute later another wave of water washed over her as he sat right down beside her on her left.

His dark hair glistened with water. Drops clung to his eyelashes.

"Now do you want to go skinny-dipping?"

"No need, I'm soaked." She glanced at him. "Next time I'll bring a bathing suit."

She'd have to buy one as she hadn't brought one. Did the local store carry any? Maybe she'd need a ride to Bryceville.

"Spoilsport," he said easily.

"You must have had a great childhood," she said looking around and imagining Kirk and his friends roaming wherever they wished, safe and happy and free.

"Sure did."

"Are you an only child?"

"Only child of an only child of an only child," he said.

"So no cousins to play with."

"Plenty of others around."

"Do your parents live in Smoky Hollow?"

"There's only my granddad. He's still here. He raised me."

Angelica swished her hands through the water, letting the cool liquid drip when she raised her palms. She remembered that's what the store owner had said.

"I should get home. I'll need to change before Sam comes," she said slowly.

She looked at Kirk. "Thanks for the picnic and bringing me here. This is such a lovely place."

He nodded in acknowledgment, then leaned over and brushed his lips against hers. It was a momentary touch which was over far, far too soon in Angelica's opinion. She felt an explosion of feelings, indescribably exquisite, with merely that brief contact.

Without a word, he rose and offered his hand to pull her up. His touch seemed electric. Water streamed from them both as she snatched her hand back and looked everywhere except at him.

He kissed her!

Her heart pounded. She wanted to touch her lips with her fingers, stop a moment and savor the feelings that roiled inside.

Instead, she turned and stepped back on the path, her shoes squishing. She knew she'd be uncomfortable all the way home. But that didn't faze her. It was that brief kiss that dominated her mind.

She didn't know how to react. Should she say something? Ignore it. Laugh it off. Her back to Kirk, she wrung water from her shirt, pulling it away from her body. Her pants were dripping at every step, her shoes dribbling water as she walked.

Taking a breath, she turned. Kirk had taken off his shirt and was wringing it out. She almost caught her breath at his masculine beauty. She knew his shoulders were broad and muscular. He looked like some kind of perfect male form that artists would long to paint. His skin was tanned and taut over muscles in his chest and flat stomach. She was mesmerized. It wasn't like she hadn't seen men in swimming trunks or something, but none she could remember looked like Kirk.

When he donned the damp shirt, she was disappointed. But she hoped he never suspected.

"Ready?" he asked.

She nodded, and followed him as he led the way along the stream and back to the picnic area. This outing was the most spontaneous fun she ever remembered.

And his kiss was not something she'd ever forget.

By the time they reached Webb Francis's home, her feet felt rubbed raw from walking in wet shoes and socks. Her shirt and cotton pants had dried for the most part, but she couldn't wait to get them off.

"Next time bring a bathing suit," he suggested as they parted.

She hesitated a moment, then nodded. Sounded like he planned on a next time. She wanted to nail that down, but still feeling awkward about that kiss, she just waved goodbye and turned to enter the cottage. She had not been expecting another kiss.

Chapter Five

Hurrying to take a quick shower and put on dry clothes, Angelica barely had her hair dry by the time Sam knocked on the door. With him was a girl of about the same age.

"Hi, Miss Cannon. This is Teresa Ann. Can you teach her to play the fiddle, too?"

"Hello, Teresa Ann. You want me to teach her in time for the festival?"

Angelica was startled that Sam had brought another child. Was Webb Francis the local music teacher?

Teresa Ann giggled.

"Not for the festival. Not this year. But if I could learn, I could play next year. My mother said I was to tell you if you take me on, she can pay five dollars a lesson. But I have to use Webb Francis's fiddle. We can't spring for one of those," Teresa Ann said.

"I see. I'm not really giving lessons," Angelica said slowly.

At the disappointment in Teresa Ann's face, she relented. "Tell you what. I'll call Webb Francis and make sure it's all right with him if you use one of his fiddles and then I'll show you the basics. He'll be home soon and then he can teach you."

"He'll say yes," Sam said. "He wants us to learn."

Angelica settled her two students on the porch with a glass of milk each and dashed over to Kirk's house. She rapped on the front door and he opened it a moment later.

"I need to talk to Webb Francis," she said, glancing back at her house to make sure the children were still sitting there.

"Right now?"

He followed her line of sight and smiled.

"Doubled your class, did you?"

"I didn't expect Sam to bring a friend. She wants to use one of Webb Francis's fiddles. I need to make sure that's all right with him."

"Sure to be. Come in and we'll call the hospital."

Five minutes later Angelica led two children into the music room.

"We'll start Sam practicing his song then I'll show you how to get started," she said to Teresa Ann.

She wasn't sure how she would manage two very different levels at the same time, but she was willing to try.

The time flew by. Sam stopped practicing from time to time to listen as Angelica explained to Teresa Ann the proper way to hold the violin and the bow. Then with a glance from Angelica, he'd begin practicing again.

An hour passed quickly and Angelica decided that was enough of lesson time for both the children. She was surprised how much fun she'd had with such rank beginners.

"You did well, Teresa Ann," she said, wiping the violin and putting it in the stand Webb Francis had for it.

"And you, Sam, are going to be the star of the festival. You're really coming along. Just keep practicing."

Both children grinned.

"You tell your mother that lessons are once a week, but practice is every day. No charge for practices." She suspected money was tight with the girl's family and didn't want to deny her the chance to learn because of finances. Webb Francis could make other arrangements when he returned and took over.

"Every day?" Teresa Ann's eyes widened.

"Not on the weekend," Angelica clarified. "And only for about a half hour. Can you do that?"

Both children nodded solemnly.

"Thanks, Miss Cannon," Sam said.

"Thank you, Miss Cannon," Teresa Ann echoed.

Both children ran out and down the road, laughing and talking about how they'd surprise everyone when they won the festival competition.

Angelica finished tidying up the music room and went to get a glass of iced tea. She'd had as much fun as the children. Maybe she had a talent for teaching as well as playing.

She'd never forget the look of sheer delight Teresa Ann had displayed when she'd played a short beginner's tune. Angelica could remember her own delight when she played a song. It had seemed like magic way back when.

So when had it become more drudgery than joy?

She was just tired and jaded from the hectic schedule over the last few years. This vacation was just what she needed.

During the afternoon, she'd spotted a CD player in Webb Francis's music room. Of course he'd have one. Now she could borrow CDs from the library and listen at home.

By the time she returned from picking up a selection of music it was late enough to prepare dinner. She'd eat it on the porch, listening to the quiet of the Kentucky evening. She had plenty to think about.

The next morning Angelica had scarcely started her coffee when there was a knock on the back door. Kirk stood on the back stoop.

"Come with me this morning. We're working on the barn and there'll be others there you can meet. Gina's the chair of the festival this year. She's worked with Webb Francis in the past. You can meet her , too," he said.

This morning he wore another T-shirt and faded jeans, with sturdy work shoes on his feet. His intense gaze had her heart turning flip-flops even as she tried to convince herself it was merely so he could understand her when she spoke.

"I can't build a barn," she said.

He laughed. "No one's asking you to. There's a potluck lunch, so you can meet people."

"I should bring something, then."

"Nope, taken care of. Are you coming or not?"

She hesitated only a moment.

"Coming. Do we leave now?"

"In about twenty minutes."

"I'll be ready. What do I wear or bring?"

He looked her over from head to toe and grinned.

"Wear what you have on and bring a hat if you have one. Otherwise you'll just have to find shade. I'll be back in twenty."

She drank her coffee in record time, eating two pieces of toast with cheese. All she had time for when she heard the truck drive round to the back of the house. She dashed out before Kirk could get out and went around to climb into the passenger seat.

"That was fast," he commented as he backed out to the road.

"You said twenty."

"Some people take that to mean more or less—like a half hour more or less."

She didn't answer, but looked eagerly around as he drove. She loved the forested road embraced by trees as they drove through. When they suddenly were in an area of cleared farmland, she looked back. The line of trees marched left and right as far as she could see. And ahead, acres and acres of corn.

"That's an abrupt change," she said. "From forest to farmland."

"Cleared several generations ago. It's a constant chore, to keep the trees from encroaching."

She saw the farmhouse and framed barn when they turned down a driveway. Cars and trucks were parked every which way in front of the house. There was one large oak tree sheltering the front yard.

"They kept one for shade," she murmured, watching the activity in the yard.

Kirk drove around the side of the house. A long trestle table had been set up beneath some large umbrellas. A few bowls of food were sitting on the table beneath netting. Plenty of room ready for the rest of the food that was sure to come.

A group of men were talking, two already climbing ladders to start in on roofing.

"Come with me," Kirk said when he parked.

He introduced her to Carrie Cooper, who with her husband Ben, owned the farm. He took off for the barn while Angelica stayed with Carrie. Her hostess introduced her to everyone as they arrived. By midmorning, there had to be more than fifty people around—men working on the barn, women fussing with food, children laughing as they raced around the yard.

Angelica felt a bit overwhelmed with all the names and faces and at one point stepped away from the crowd a little. She searched the men on the barn, finding Kirk with no trouble. He was on top of the roof, swinging his hammer with precision. She caught her breath for a moment, wondering what kept him anchored on the steep pitch. It looked as if he could slide off with no trouble.

Carrie joined her, looking in the same direction.

"We're lucky to have him, you know," she said.

"Oh?"

Angelica didn't move her gaze. He looked amazing, all muscles and broad shoulders and tanned skin. She swallowed.

"He knows so much about construction. We'd have had to hire a contractor if Kirk didn't donate his time and expertise. Our old barn burned, you know."

Carrie studied Kirk for a moment.

"Actually, we're all lucky he survived the mortar attack."

"Where he lost his hearing?"

"Yes. And then I didn't think he'd come back to Smoky Hollow. I mean, what is there here for a single guy? Not a lot of women, not a lot of business around, you know? Farming's our biggest industry. His granddaddy farms, but Kirk never took to it like old man Devon wanted."

"You've known him a long time," Angelica said, looking at her hostess.

Here was someone who could tell her more about the man who so intrigued her.

"We went to school together. He was a grade ahead of me and one behind Ben. Wild and fun, that was Kirk."

She smiled in remembrance.

"I've got to get back to the mob. Don't let us overwhelm you. Kirk said you wanted to know more about the music festival. Gina just arrived. Come meet her. You two can talk about the festival. She'll love a fresh ear, you know."

Angelica and Gina clicked instantly. They both loved music, though different forms. Angelica knew she could learn a lot from her. When Gina discovered she was giving lessons to two children, she eagerly asked if Angelica would consider giving more. Was the fiddle the only thing she could teach? What was she charging?

Before she could answer, Kirk walked up.

"You two eating?" he asked. He'd put on his shirt and taken off his cap.

Angelica looked around. Everyone had a plate, either eating or still in line along the trestle table, piling food on.

"Hey, Kirk. You're looking good," Gina said, giving him a hug.

He grinned at Gina.

"Don't let your husband hear you flirting with me, I don't want to have to fend him off."

She laughed.

"It'll be our secret. I'm so happy to meet Angelica. She said you're helping her get acquainted around town."

"Standing in for Webb Francis. He'll take over once he's back."

Angelica refused to let her smile wobble, but the comment hurt. She'd thought he'd done more than stand in for the older man.

Rising, she avoided Kirk's eyes and headed for the table.

"It looks like a feast," she said with as much enthusiasm as she could muster.

She needed to remember why she was here. It wasn't to flirt with Kirk Devon.

He stood behind her in line.

"Meet everybody?" he asked as she added some salad to her plate.

"Yes, thank you."

She moved on to one of the casseroles.

"You going to play in the festival?"

"Probably not."

She moved on, wishing someone would engage Kirk in conversation. She didn't want him to feel he had to stick with her.

"Why not?"

"My type of music isn't really what people down here want to hear."

"Music's music," he murmured.

She glanced at his plate. It looked as if it held enough food to feed a family of four.

"Are you going to eat all that?" she asked, startled.

Compared to his plate, hers looked like it belonged to an anorexic.

"You going to eat only that?" he countered. "You're going to hurt some feelings if you don't have a helping of most everything."

She blinked, then began taking a spoonful from each dish. "Better?"

"Only if you eat it as well," he said, pushing against her a little.

The touch zinged through her like lightning. She felt her knees grow weak.

"Don't push," she whispered.

"Say again?" he said, leaning closer to hear her.

She stared into his dark brown eyes, awareness spiking to an all-time high. She wanted to drop her plate, put her arms around him and kiss him until she forgot her name.

Sanity returned. She stepped along, stopping to get a glass of the ubiquitous iced tea and then looking for a place to sit.

"Gina saved us places," Kirk said by her right ear.

She spotted her new friend waving and headed in that direction. "You don't have to babysit me all day," she said to Kirk.

"No hardship on my part," he replied easily.

Then he greeted others at the long picnic table.

Gina made introductions to the people Angelica hadn't met. When the conversation turned to music, Angelica took notice. It sounded like the festival would be exactly what she was looking for. And she could easily stay until the end of August, the money she'd brought would stretch that far—especially as she was living for free right now in Webb Francis's house.

After lunch, the men resumed their work on the structure. The roof was on, siding going up, and inside she could hear hammering and sawing. Once the food had been put away, or carried off by those having to leave early, Angelica walked over to the barn, peering inside to see what was going on there.

It wasn't as bright as in the sunshine, so it took her a few minutes to get used to the dimness. Spotting Kirk using a table saw, she carefully walked over.

He cut board after board while one of the men stacked the pieces until he had several, then carried them over to where she could see they were separating space with stalls.

Kirk looked over and saw her.

"I came to see what you were doing," she said.

He tilted his head slightly.

"This wood is for the stalls, isn't it?" she asked.

"We'll do as much as we can today. I think we'll finish if everyone working stays until it's done."

"Carrie said you're donating your time and expertise," she said watching as different men did different tasks. It looked like a choreographed production.

"All of us are donating time for this. Traditions like that go back to the founding of the country. Ben bought the material, we're just putting it together."

She nodded, trying to find a similar situation in her own life where people gave freely of time and ability and got nothing in return except the satisfaction of helping a neighbor. Granted, her parents donated to charities, but never put themselves out beyond that to help.

Neither had she, she realized with some shame. There must have been some time she had, but nothing came to mind.

Except—maybe the children who had come to her at Webb Francis's house. She hadn't wanted to give them lessons, but Kirk had seen it as something to do. She didn't have to accept money from Teresa Ann's mother. She could teach her and Sam for nothing. She thought about it for a minute. She wasn't a teacher, yet she could share some of what she knew. How hard would it be to give a little of her knowledge to two children so thirsty to learn? She couldn't build a barn, but she could help two children who would otherwise not have lessons until Webb Francis was back.

"Excuse me, miss," one man said, reaching around her to take the freshly sawed board.

"I think I'm in the way," she said.

"Stand over there if you want to watch for a while. You and Gina talked out?"

She nodded.

"She had to leave. I know more about the festival now. And how I can help Sam better. He wants to play in it."

She wanted to share her newly made decision about teaching the boy, but now was not the time. Instead, she watched as Kirk swiftly measured lengths of lumber, drew a straight line cross the grain and then sawed through in a second. As fast as he cut, others would take up the board and place it between stalls and hammer them in. The men moved smoothly as if they'd worked together before and knew each others' routine.

"They make it look easy," she said.

"It is, once you know what you're doing," he said, then the saw screamed again as it bit through the wood.

"You've done this before, then," she said at another quiet moment.

He nodded, without stopping.

"I saw America working my way through building projects."

Another cut, another board. When Angelica looked at the stall, it was almost complete. Framing was going up for another. As Kirk had said, the barn would be completed today, she suspected. The men of Smoky Hollow had done an amazing amount of work in one day.

"I think I'll catch a ride back to the library," she said a minute later.

With her new decision, she wanted to see if there were any books that might give her a hint of how to teach children music.

"Take my truck."

He paused long enough to fish the keys out of his pocket and tossed them to her. They were still warm from his body. She clenched them tightly in her hand, wondering if she could drive that truck. It looked larger than the car she drove when in Boston.

"Turn right out of the driveway and keep on until you reach the library. You know the way home from there," he said, selecting another board.

"How will you get back?"

"I'll hitch a ride." He looked at her. "Or you can come back in a couple of hours and pick me up."

"I can come back after four. Sam's coming over today to practice. And maybe Teresa Ann."

"Your class is growing."

She shrugged. It wasn't really a class, just a couple of kids who wanted to learn—as she had back when she'd been their age.

"I'll be back after four."

"I'll be here."

Angelica stopped at the yard to tell Carrie goodbye and let her know she'd be back for Kirk.

"One day we'll have to have lunch and you can tell me all about New York. I've never been, seems a long ways from here. But that doesn't mean I don't want to know everything."

Others called out to her as she was leaving, smiling and waving. She felt a curious connection after only one day with the people she'd met.

It was closer to five than four when Angelica turned back into the driveway. The barn looked complete. She wasn't sure how the inside fared, but the only thing left on the outside was to paint it. There were men sprawled everywhere in the yard, obviously tired and relaxing after a full day of work. She spotted Kirk instantly. He sat on the ground, one leg bent, his arm resting on his knee. He was talking with two other men, each with a beer in hand. He must have heard the truck because he turned.

Angelica was caught by his smile when he saw her. She pulled to a stop short of the group and opened the door. Almost before she was on the ground, he was there. He looked hot. She swallowed as her senses revved up around him, wishing she had the right to reach out and touch, hold on to him, feel his arms around her in a hug.

Blinking, she slid along the side of the truck, hoping she wasn't giving away the fascination she had.

"Nary a scratch or dent," she said, pushing against her inclination to step closer, and continuing to move toward the back.

"I didn't expect one," he said easily.

"Ready to leave?" she asked.

"I am. I'm beat. But we're finished. A couple of guys are coming on Saturday to paint. Jason has a sprayer, should be able to complete it in a day. But that's not my thing."

He stepped closer.

She stepped back.

"I'll get in the truck, then."

And she almost ran around to the passenger door.

Kirk watched her, then with a wave and a shout goodbye, he climbed into the truck. The ride home was in silence.

Angelica clasped her hands tightly, as if holding on to her roiling emotions. She needed to get a grip. She was here to temporarily escape a life becoming too stressful and frenetic. She'd be leaving at the end of summer.

After talking with Gina, she was determined to stay for the music festival. It sounded like an event not to be missed to hear more of the folk music of Appalachia.

"How is Sam doing?" Kirk asked when he almost reached her driveway.

"He's doing very well. I think he'll be ready for the festival. And Teresa Ann loves playing. Even chords. I can see the delight shining in her eyes."

"I know they appreciate your helping out."

"Does Webb Francis give lessons?" she asked.

"When kids ask. He mostly plays for himself these days. He taught at the university for a while. But he's retired now."

He pulled into her driveway and stopped and looked at her.

"Are you going to play in the festival?" he asked.

"I think I might. I've been thinking about it since talking with Gina. I want to try some of the mountain music. Any favorites?"

He studied her for a moment.

"Orange Blossom Special, but it's a hard one. Do you think you can play it the way it should be played?"

Was he throwing that out as a challenge? She'd heard the song before, she knew how complex it was, and how fast it was played. Could she do it?

"Maybe I'll work on that for you," she said, opening the door. "Thanks for taking me today. I enjoyed meeting everyone and talking with Gina. Next time, I can bring some food. I do know how to cook."

"Good to know."

She walked into the house hearing the truck pull out. Pausing at the door, she watched as it turned into his place and was lost from sight when it went to the far side of his cabin.

Scanning the sky she wished for another storm. But the sky was a cloudless blue. No excuse to go to her neighbor's for dinner today.

Kirk quickly showered and made a hasty dinner. After eating, he headed for his studio. He was tired after the day's work, but still anxious to get going on the new carving he'd thought about all day. He had just the block of wood for it, a huge center of an oak that had to be almost four feet across. He'd had it a few years, not knowing what he wanted to do with it. Now he did.

It took block and tackle to get it moved over to the center of the room. Too tall to put on the table; he'd have to work on it on the floor. Studying it from all angles, he then sketched out the outline of the image he had in mind. Then penciled the overall shape on the side to know where to start carving. In only moments, he was completely caught up in the wood, the tools and the vision.

It was late when he straightened and realized how tired he was. He'd made a start, however. It wasn't easy using oak, much harder wood than others he used. But the lines in this were perfect. The shape of trees and a figure on the edge of a cliff were roughed in. It would take weeks to get it the way he saw it in his mind. Enough for tonight. He needed to get some sleep.

Crossing the distance to his house, he glanced at the house next door. Would he finish it before Angelica left? If he worked at it full time he could. Did he want her to see it? It was the most personal thing he'd ever carved.

And he wasn't sure he could capture the expression on the face—awestruck, delight, freedom. Maybe that's what he'd call it—freedom.

The next morning the phone rang while Kirk was still eating breakfast.

"Hi Kirk, it's Webb Francis," the voice on the other end said.

"How's it going? You coming home today?"

He waited a moment while the older man coughed.

"Not coming home for a while. My sister heard I was sick and is planning for me to stay with her in Louisville until I'm fit again. I may get discharged from the hospital later this week. Here's hoping. How're things there?"

"Fine. You're missed. Gina especially wants to talk to you more about the festival. Speaking of which, your guest plans to play in it after all."

"Angelica Cannon, that's wonderful. She's a rare talent. From what I hear she's played as a soloist in the New York Philharmonic already at her young age. And some of her solo concerts have been reviewed to high accolades. She's the reason I'm calling."

"Did you call your house?"

"I tried there earlier, no answer. I was feeling better yesterday so I called Ryan Simmons."

Kirk tried to remember anyone he knew by that name.

"Do I know him?"

"No, he was Angelica's professor at the conservatory. He's been trying to reach her, but her cell isn't on—or not working in Smoky Hollow more like. Anyway, can you let her know he needs to talk to her. She can use my phone, don't worry about the cost. She learning anything?"

"I don't know about that, but she's borrowed a stack of CDs from the library and seems to be faithfully working with those kids each afternoon."

"They'll learn a lot from her. Wish I could be there, but Betsy is so adamant about my coming to her place, she's threatened to send Charles to wrestle me there if I don't go on my own."

"Let her fatten you up. As I remember, Betsy's a great cook."

"Yes, just what I need." He coughed again. "Sorry to ask you to keep an eye on my place longer."

"That's what neighbors are for, you know that. Anyway, Angelica is melding in fine. She's leaving after the festival."

If he said it often enough, he'd remember it—and keep that fact in the forefront of his mind. She'd looked good enough to eat when she arrived yesterday afternoon at Carrie and Ben's. But by the way she'd almost run around the truck and then dashed into the house when they reached it, she didn't share that growing awareness whenever she was around.

He was having a hard time remembering she was only visiting.

"Figured she'd only stay a little while. She has a career in New York. I'm sorry I can't play with her. I bet that would be something."

"Your sister's care will have you recovering quickly. You might make the festival—play a duet or something," Kirk said.

"We'll see. Tell her to call Professor Simmons."

Kirk replaced the receiver after the call. He wanted to get to work on the new carving, but it wouldn't take long to give her the message.

Chapter Six

He walked across the lawn between the two houses noting again that Webb Francis's lawn needed mowing. Maybe he'd get to that later today. It'd be dry enough after the rain. He went to the back door and knocked. Angelica opened it and gave that smile that made her the prettiest woman he'd ever seen.

"Come in. Want some coffee?"

He hesitated. He was only going to give her the message and then leave. But might as well be neighborly.

"Sure. I heard from Webb Francis earlier."

"Sit down. How's he doing?"

She began to bustle around the kitchen, measuring the grounds then pouring boiling water over them in the French press.

"He's doing better, though he sounds awful on the phone. He's going to his sister's when discharged, which he thinks will be later this week."

"Oh." She stopped and turned around. "Does that mean I should leave?"

"No, he likes having someone here watching the place."

"Sure, like there's any danger. No one even locks their doors."

"Well, better to be lived in than not. He had a message for you. Call Professor Simmons. Apparently the man's been trying to reach you but your cell doesn't work here."

"I haven't even turned it on since I arrived. I wonder what he wants."

"Call and find out," he suggested.

"Okay, if you don't mind. The coffee will be ready in a couple of minutes."

She reached for the kitchen phone and punched in the numbers. She asked to speak to the professor, but he was in class. She gave the local phone number for him to call.

"That told me nothing," she said when she poured the coffee into two mugs. "Do you take anything in yours?"

"No, I like it black and hot."

She set the mug in front of him and sat across the table.

"Tell me about some of the other buildings you've worked on," she said.

"What brought that on?"

"I was thinking of how you knew how to do everything with that barn, from the roof to the stalls to framing. I noticed others checked with you as if you were the boss or something."

"Something. I've built a few buildings in my time."

"Working your way around America."

He nodded, sipping the hot coffee and looking at her. Her voice was borderline too soft to hear. He really had to concentrate, but that was no hardship. She looked bright and rested today. He still thought she should put on a few more pounds, she was thinner than any woman he knew. Her cheeks were pink and her eyes a bright blue, as if the sun-kissed color in her face enhanced them. A few more days in the sunshine and she'd stop looking like she just got out of a hospital or something.

"So is that how you make a living, building things?"

"You could say that."

She waited a moment, then took a sip of her own coffee.

"Do you play an instrument?"

He shook his head. "Someone has to be the audience."

She smiled at that. "Will you come to the festival?"

"I'll probably be there part of the time."

The part where she played. He didn't hear well enough at the outdoor concerts to stay long. But he'd get a front row seat to hear her.

"I listened to a song last night that I had a hard time understanding the words. It was a ballad and sounded like half the words are ones I don't know."

"Probably old English. There are a few sad songs sung that harken back to the early days."

"So can anyone translate for me so I know what they're saying?" she asked.

He thought a moment.

"Webb Francis. Gina. My granddad."

"Your grandfather? Does he play an instrument?"

"No. But he had a terrific voice. Used to sing at all the festivals. Hasn't in the last twenty years or so, but he knows all the songs."

"Why did he stop?"

"He had a falling out with the woman in charge of the festival that year. Never went back."

"Wooo, he holds a grudge."

Kirk nodded.

"Do you think he'd help me?"

"Worth a shot. I'll take you over this morning and you can try for yourself."

He wondered what reaction his grandfather would have to Angelica. He had never had many friends and hadn't come to town much in recent months. But he used to love to sing. Who had he hurt most by his refusal to sing in the festival, Kirk wondered.

It was after ten when Kirk and Angelica arrived at the farm where Kirk had grown up.

"This is so pretty," Angelica said as they drove down rows of corn bordering the drive. "When is the harvest?" She studied the tall plants noting the ears were clearly visible and looked as large as any she'd ever eaten.

"Starts next month."

"And where does all this corn go?"

"We put up some. Locals buy it from Granddad and the rest is for the hogs."

"Hogs?"

"That's my grandfather's primary money-maker. Hogs."

When he pulled into the yard surrounding the house, Angelica noted the old homestead was made of wood, freshly painted and looking solid and enduring. Behind the house was a barn, smaller than the one she'd seen built. It was painted a rust color red. The huge double doors stood wide open. From inside she could hear the squeal of hogs. The noise was almost deafening. A hound dog ran from the barn. Angelica wondered how it could have heard the truck over the noise of the animals.

"Late feeding this morning," Kirk commented.

He went around the truck and opened her door, then gestured toward the barn. "Want to see?"

She nodded, falling in step as he headed that way, petting the dog as he trotted next to them, tail wagging.

Inside the barn was lit by overhead lights. Stalls lined each side of the wide center aisle, but whereas the horse barn had high walls, these were only about four feet high. The sound hurt her ears and she covered them.

An older man was near the end, dumping meal into a trough. The hogs in that stall were standing on their hind legs, front braced against the wooden stall door, squealing in delight. To the right all the hogs had been fed, they were snorting and pushing into the food troughs eating as if they hadn't had food in a month. To the left, only two stalls had hogs waiting to eat. Without a speck of patience among them.

Fascinated, Angelica kept pace with Kirk, her hands blocking some of the high-pitched sounds.

Kirk's grandfather turned and saw them, but didn't pause in his task of feeding. When the last one had been fed he turned and spoke.

"This Webb Francis's guest?" he asked.

She dropped her hands now that the noise had ceased. Smiling politely she waited while Kirk made introductions.

"It is. Angelica, this is my grandfather, Hiram Devon. This is Angelica Cannon from New York."

"Humph. How long you here for?"

She was surprised at the lack of greeting. Everyone else in Smoky Hollow had been friendly.

"Until after the music festival. I heard that you sing."

"Not any more."

He turned and walked to the feed bin, hanging the bucket beside it.

"I'm learning more about folk music," she said. "A song I heard yesterday has me puzzled. I couldn't understand all the words. Kirk said you might know what they are and what they mean."

He frowned. His gray hair was covered by a beat-up old felt hat. His bushy iron-gray eyebrows almost met over his nose.

"What song?"

"The Alder Tree?"

He nodded. "I know it."

Angelica didn't know if she should push to have him help her or if it would be better to let him decide without any pressure.

"What else you need doing this morning?" Kirk asked.

"Still have to check the water in each trough, open the doors so they can get out if they want."

"I'll do that if you want to tell Angelica the words," he said.

The man studied her for another moment, then nodded.

"Guess I could."

Angelica followed Hiram Devon into the old kitchen through the mudroom where he toed off his muddy boots and slipped into regular shoes. She looked around, curious to see the home in which Kirk had grown up. She'd seen his home now, with its modern touches and homey feel. This place looked worn and old, but it was scrupulously clean.

"Want anything?" he asked, as he went to wash his hands.

"Nothing, thanks," she replied, taking a seat at the wooden table and pulling a notebook from her tote. "I tried to write down the words as I heard them, and tried to figure them out on my own."

He took the notebook and scanned what she'd written.

With a sigh, he took the offered pen and began writing next to her lines wherever she had it wrong.

Angelica studied him as he worked, trying to see a resemblance to Kirk in the older man's features. Maybe in the eyes.

He looked up and caught her staring.

She looked away, not wanting to offend or have him stop helping.

"There, those are the words. The song came over from the

old country generations ago. It's about a young man leaving Scotland to go to America and the girl and friends he left behind. When word of his death reaches them, there's mourning in the entire village."

"How sad."

He shrugged. "Life was tough in those days."

"So what exactly does this word mean?"

For several minutes she jotted down the meaning of the words she didn't know. He hummed the tune while she tried to match words to melody. "I could play this on the violin—fiddle, I mean."

"You probably could. It's not hard."

"If I do, would you sing it with me so I know I have it right?"

"Here?"

"I can bring my violin here. Or you could come to Webb Francis's home."

"I don't get into town much. You come here. Practice up and let me know when you're ready."

"Thank you, Mr. Devon. I really appreciate this."

"We'll see how you do. Why are you interested in all this? I thought you played in the New York symphony."

"I do. I'm taking a break and wanted to explore some different music. When I had a class in folk music at the conservatory, I really liked it and wanted to learn more."

"So you just up and came here. For how long?"

"Several weeks. Until after the music festival."

"Humph. Kirk know you aren't staying?"

"Of course. Everyone does. I didn't move here. I'm only on vacation, a sort of working vacation as it were."

He nodded, looked toward the back door. In another moment, Kirk entered. He kicked off his motorcycle boots and walked in the kitchen in his sock feet.

"All set. Were you able to help Angelica?" he asked, going to the sink to wash his hands.

"Told her the words and what they mean," Hiram said.

"Once I think I've mastered the melody on the violin—fiddle—he's going to sing it for me," she said.

"Is that so?"

He looked with surprise at his grandfather.

"I said I would. She can come here when she thinks she's ready."

Kirk pulled out the chair next to her and sat in it.

"How did you pull that off?" he asked softly, looking directly at her.

"I just asked," she said, drawing in a breath, caught by his fabulous good looks and the intense way he regarded her.

She could smell the hint of hogs. She stared back, feeling the fluttering inside that had her craving more. Would he ever kiss her again?

"I had a good voice when I was younger," Hiram said.

She started a second with the surprise of his comment. Tearing her eyes away from Kirk, she looked at the older man.

"I bet you still do," she said.

"Tell me about New York. I haven't been there for years."

Kirk looked at him. "When were you in New York?"

"Back after your dad took off with your mom. I went to see a play that a friend of Webb Francis wrote. Saw the Statue of Liberty and some other sights. Crowded, dirty, busy. Didn't like it much. It was a sight to see Broadway at night, though. Gotta admit that was something."

Angelica smiled.

"It's still something, all lighted up as bright as day. Plays and concerts, restaurants and bars. Lots of activity. If you were there thirty years or so ago, I bet it's changed some."

"I bet it's still crowded, dirty and busy."

She nodded.

"Central Park on a nice day is wonderful. I love to eat along the battery, near the water, watching people. And shopping can't be beat."

Kirk leaned back in his chair and watched as his grandfather and Angelica talked about New York. She kind of lit up when talking about the things she liked to do in the city.

It was a good reminder she was on vacation in Smoky Hollow. A woman who had spent years in America's most dynamic city would never settle down in rural Kentucky. Look at Alice. She'd been born and raised here and couldn't wait to leave.

He needed to heed the signs. Any attraction could go nowhere, so squash it at the get-go. She was beautiful, more so when animated and excited about her topic. He'd be lucky to score a few kisses, maybe another couple of outings together.

Webb Francis wanted him to keep an eye on her. But he couldn't let her come to mean more than a casual visitor. He'd tried forever after and lost. Maybe one day he'd be attracted to another woman who would be content living in Smoky Hollow. But Angelica Cannon was not the one.

Suddenly he realized both of them were staring at him.

"What?"

"You in a fog, boy? I asked about Webb Francis."

"Sorry. I didn't hear you."

It was a pathetic excuse but better than letting either know he was steeling himself to ignore the attraction he felt around the pretty visitor.

"He's going to his sister's to finish recuperating. She's insisting."

"Family rallies around when needed," Hiram said.

When they left a short time later, Angelica had her translation in hand.

"I appreciate your grandfather helping me," she told Kirk as they drove off.

She turned for one last glimpse of the house and the dog lying in the dirt looking like he'd lost his best friend.

"That surprises me. He's usually more standoffish with strangers. He likes Smoky Hollow to be old residents, I think. Not that he goes to town that much."

"Why not?"

"He's feuding with half the town it seems like."

"Apparently not Webb Francis, he asked after him."

"They get along fine. Hope Webb Francis makes the festival. It shouldn't be that hard to sit and enjoy the music. Betsy would have to bring him."

"Is she the sister? It must be nice to have family around in times of need."

He flicked her a glance.

"Aren't yours?"

"I'm sure they would. But sometimes too much of a good thing can be smothering."

"Want to get a bite to eat at the diner?" he asked as they reached town.

"I'd like that."

Seated in a red vinyl booth a few minutes later, Angelica was reading the menu when an older woman stopped by.

"Hey, Kirk. How are you?"

He half rose and nodded.

"Miz Harper. I'm doing fine. Yourself?"

"Arthritis acting up, but that's nothing new."

She looked at Angelica.

Kirk made introductions.

"Heard from Alice the other day. She and her husband were going to the Caribbean for vacation. Sure wish she'd settled here."

"Yes, ma'am, I reckon we all do," he said.

Angelica watched the interaction between the two struck by the tension that appeared. Was there more to that statement than appeared?

When the woman left, Angelica leaned forward so he could hear her, but so no one else in the diner could.

"Who was that?"

He looked after Mrs. Harper for a moment, then shrugged.

"She's Alice's mother."

"And Alice is?"

"Was—my fiancée."

Angelica blinked.

"What happened?"

He closed his menu, laid it near the edge of the table.

"She didn't want to live in Smoky Hollow. Moved to Atlanta, found another man and got married."

Angelica couldn't believe another man could compete with Kirk.

"And you didn't want to live in Atlanta?"

He shook his head.

"My granddad is here. My family's been here for generations. I like it here, why would I want to live in a city when the forest and hills offer so much?"

"Did you love her?"

"What kind of question is that? Of course I did. I wouldn't ask a woman to marry me that I didn't love. Marriage is hard enough. Especially in my family."

"Why especially in your family?"

"My granddad's wife left when my dad was a kid. My own mother left when I was still a baby. And then Alice left. Not good odds, do you think?"

"All left because they didn't want to live in Smoky Hollow?" she asked in disbelief.

He shook his head. The waitress came over to take their orders. When she'd left, Angelica leaned forward again.

"So why did they leave?"

"I don't know the full story of my grandmother, but my granddad isn't the easiest man in the world to get along with. She ran off to be an actress in Hollywood. Had a few two-bit parts that I know about and then nothing. No one knows what happened to her. She could still be living there or could have died years ago."

"And your mother?"

"She decided she didn't want to raise a child. She went to New Orleans where last I heard she's part owner of a small restaurant near the Quarter."

"You never see her?"

He shook his head.

"I looked her up a few years ago when I was traveling. But there was no instant bonding or strong family ties. She was a stranger and viewed me as one as well. She can cook, though. I had the best meal in a long time at that restaurant where she's head chef as well as the part owner."

"Your dad and grandfather never found other women to marry?"

"Once bitten, twice shy."

"And you?"

"Oh, I expect I'll find someone one day. I'd like to have a kid or two. But I want a woman who loves living here. Who wants the same things I do, who will be content here in Smoky Hollow. Someone who puts family above all else. Not looking for fame or a fast lifestyle."

"Nice, if you can get it," she said.

"And if I don't, I'm content with the way things are going now."

"Except no kids."

"There is that."

She was silent for a moment. Trying to see into her own future. She had never met a man she wanted to spend her life with. Most of the men she dated were older, more patrons of the arts than looking for a wife.

In one case, she might have had a chance as a second wife. But Marshall had not made her heart flutter and after only a few dates they stopped seeing each other. She was young yet, she didn't feel any urgency to get married. Now she wanted to explore more of the world before getting tied down to one man.

Looking away, she tried not to compare Kirk to those other men she'd dated. Or figure out how he could become the one. He and she would never make a couple. He lived here. Her life was in New York. And from the way he spoke of Alice, the thought of living in a big city never crossed his mind. He seemed to let her go easily enough. Had he really loved her? Had he been devastated when she left?

She'd never fantasized about getting married. Did she even want children? She'd never been much around them.

Yet, she enjoyed the encounters with Sam and Teresa Ann. And she liked looking at babies. How would it be to have a child, raise it up, teach it her values, teach it to appreciate music?

One thing for sure, she'd never pressure a child as she had been.

"You're not married, anyone on the horizon?" he asked.

She shook her head.

"I haven't dated much, except for musicians or men who love the symphony. That's going to have to change. I don't want nothing else in my life. I want variety and change and something different."

Looking around at the diner, she smiled.

"This is different."

"Not trendy like New York."

"Maybe not, but still very nice. Everyone seems to know everyone. That's definitely different from New York. I like it."

When the waitress brought their burgers, fries and sodas, Angelica ate with relish. She didn't have to rush through meals in order to make an appointment or a rehearsal. She could eat what she wanted, enjoy every mouthful.

Then take her time deciding what to do next.

"These are great," she said a few minutes later.

"Different. Variety," he said.

She grinned. "Right you are."

After lunch they drove to the store so she could pick up a few items. The two old men sat in the rockers.

"Afternoon, Miss Cannon," one said.

"Good afternoon. What's happened around here today?" she asked, pausing on the porch.

The men gave her an update of who had been shopping that morning, who was at the library and the rumors that were going around about her playing at the festival.

"I might just do that," she said. "I've been practicing," she confided, leaning closer as if conveying a secret.

"Do tell, what will you play?"

"The fiddle, of course."

"What song?"

"Ah, you'll have to come to the festival to see," she said, enjoying the exchange.

These men were delightful. And for a few minutes she almost felt as if she belonged.

"Where is the festival held?" she asked Kirk as they entered the store. Bella greeted them. Angelica waved and took a cart for her groceries.

"At the county fairgrounds. It's always scheduled after the county fair which kicked off yesterday. There's a kind of amphitheater where the acoustics are good. Those who don't get there early enough, or have small kids, usually sit on the lawn around the stage."

"Show me sometime."

"Sure."

He studied her for a moment.

"We can go to the fair tomorrow if you want, see it with all that's going on there. It's not far. Between here and Bryceville."

She nodded. "I've never been to a county fair."

"That doesn't surprise me. We'll leave around ten, have lunch there, wander around and see everything."

"Like what?"

"Future Farmers of America displays, livestock, quilts, jam and pie displays, you name it. They have music going all day in different venues around the fairgrounds, and a small carnival with rides and games. Lots to eat, too."

"Okay. I'll let my students know I won't be here tomorrow. Thanks, Kirk."

She knew he was only squiring her around as a favor to Webb Francis who was doing a favor for Professor Simmons. Still—she felt anticipation rise at the thought of the outing.

Once again she felt she was in an alien world. One she loved exploring.

Angelica was home before the two children arrived. They ran partway and were out of breath when they clattered up to her door. She set them both to work playing scales and showing Teresa Ann more techniques while Sam practiced his festival song. He was really showing signs of improvement and Angelica was proud of the child.

Teresa Ann liked to talk, but she applied herself to the tasks at hand and was already showing she had a talent for the instrument.

Angelica didn't have them play the songs she'd grown up with, but tried to incorporate the songs she was learning from the CDs and the music Webb Francis had around.

After their practice, she provided cookies and milk. She loved listening to the chatter of the two, talking about people she didn't know. When she asked what they did the rest of the summer days, she got a glimpse of their lives in Smoky Hollow—chores, playing with friends, helping at the church, exploring the creeks and woods. A slower pace of life and one that sounded idyllic.

When she explained why she wouldn't be home the next afternoon, she was surprised at the disappointment of the children.

"I love you teaching me," Teresa Ann said, giving her an unexpected hug.

"I'm enjoying teaching you, honey," Angelica said with a smile. "It's only one day. I've never been to a fair before."

Both children were astonished. They'd been going every year as long as they could remember.

"I like the rides best," Sam said. "Especially the one where we go upside down."

Teresa Ann added she liked looking at all the animals best. Both families were going on Friday and the children were looking forward to the day at the fair.

"You'll love it," Teresa Ann said. "Can I go with you, too? Then I'd have two days to go."

"Better not this time. Kirk Devon asked me so I can't invite anyone else."

"It's a date," Sam said wisely. "Kids don't go on dates."

Chapter Seven

Angelica was getting used to the casual attire she wore all the time in Smoky Hollow. She selected cotton slacks, a cotton T-shirt and comfortable walking shoes. She heard the motorcycle right at ten and went through the back door to the side of the house just as Kirk pulled up.

She kept thinking of Sam's comment—it's a date.

It was, no matter what kind of spin Kirk or she put on it. She almost danced out of the house. She was going on a date with Kirk Devon.

He greeted her, handed her the helmet then waited for her to climb on. She felt self-conscious putting her arms around him and snuggling up against his back. She knew the kiss at the pond had meant nothing to him, but the memory made her awareness spike to an all-time high.

She tried desperately to get control of her emotions. They had the entire day ahead of them. She refused to act like a silly schoolgirl with a crush. Taking a deep breath to calm her jangled nerves, she took in the scent of the man instead, kicking awareness up another notch.

He smelled of soap and aftershave and the combination did odd things to her thought processes—or lack thereof.

While she was fighting her attraction, he turned the

motorcycle around and roared out into the street heading for Bryceville and the county fairgrounds.

Angelica was glad for the end of the ride when they turned into the fairgrounds parking area. She felt tingly and self-conscious and wanted to gain some equilibrium.

Avidly looking everywhere she was immediately enchanted by what she saw. The air was filled with animal smells. The bright sunshine was already heating everything.

They parked on a dirt parking lot among pickup trucks and older model cars. Between the parking lot and the gate she saw rows of horse trailers parked every which way. She'd never seen such a sight before.

They walked to the gate where a lanky teenager stamped the back of everyone's hands once they'd paid admission.

"So we can come and go if we wish," Kirk explained. "One fee lets us into everything, including all the rides."

Angelica nodded, still trying to take in everything.

Did counties in New York have fairs like this? She'd never heard of one, but then, would she, living in New York City?

Once through the gate, Angelica saw the stables. Horses hung their heads over the stall doors and watched as people passed by. Several children went to the horses to pet them. A few owners sat on benches, working with bridles and talking with friends.

Beyond were dozens of pens covered from the hot sun by high metal roofs. Sheep were in one section, hogs in another, cattle in a third. The smell was a mix of hot dirt and the excrement of the assorted animals. Pungent and sometimes overwhelming, its earthiness had Angelica taking shallow breaths. She wrinkled her nose, but smiled. How amazing.

Kirk led the way down one aisle with sheep in small pens on either side. Some were all curly wool and a dirty white. Others had black faces and legs with snowy fleece everywhere else. Some were covered with canvas coats.

"To keep them clean for the judging," he explained when she asked why they wore covers on such a hot day.

When a group of teenagers laughingly headed their way, Kirk pulled Angelica closer, out of their path. One hand around her shoulders, he drew her against his chest. Her pulse raced. Swallowing, Angelica couldn't speak. She didn't move away once the kids had passed, content to be snuggled up against Kirk, smelling his scent mingled with that of the ambient air surrounding them. She could stay here forever.

He must have felt the same as he didn't release her, but continued to point out features of the sheep and explain the judging. She turned her head to see where he was pointing, but wished she could lay it on his shoulder and have him pull her even closer.

When he stepped forward, she moved away, walking at his side. He reached down and caught her hand, lacing his fingers with hers.

She wondered how she could concentrate on the fair with the waves of sensation washing through her.

Once out of the animal barns, there was a center walkway as wide as a street with assorted buildings on either side, like the main street of an old sleepy Southern town. Even to the rocking chairs on several porches—occupied. Some had kids rocking madly. Others had an older couple watching the people saunter by.

When Kirk ran into neighbors he knew, he introduced Angelica, explaining he was showing her around. She wished for a little while that she wasn't in Smoky Hollow merely for a visit, but could be a part of the community.

How amazing it'd be to know everyone she ran into, to stop

and chat a few minutes, knowing she'd see them again in a day or two.

The morning took on a magical feel—like something out of a fairy tale. She was enchanted with everything, from the animals to the canning and quilting, to the wonderful art exhibits. There was plenty to eat at the food court, where anything from teriyaki chicken to corn dogs to cotton candy was readily available. And sun tea booths everywhere. Which they took advantage of as the day grew warmer.

Stopping to eat lunch on the lawn near one of the platforms, they listened to the musicians playing that hour. Kirk explained how the various musical groups rotated around the fairgrounds. There were several venues where different type of music from bluegrass to country to rock were played.

"Did you put on sunscreen?" he asked as they were finishing their lunch.

She shook her head.

"Your nose is looking red," he commented. "Come on and we'll buy you a hat to keep you shaded."

She wrinkled her nose, feeling tightness.

"I didn't even think about it this morning."

She was rarely out in the sun enough to worry about sunburn at home.

However, if the feeling on her nose was anything to go by, she'd be burned to a crisp by the end of the day if she didn't do something.

Kirk led her to one of the concession stands where hats and scarves and sunglasses were sold. He picked out a pink cowboy hat and plopped it on her head.

"It's so you," he teased.

She laughed and looked at the small mirror on the stand. For a moment she didn't recognize the reflection. Her face was pink, her eyes a deeper blue than normal. But it was the happiness shining back at her that surprised her.

"We'll take it," he told the vendor, paying him for the hat.

"I can buy it," she protested, noticing the transaction.

"Consider it a gift from Smoky Hollow. I bet you don't have the nerve to wear it in New York."

She smiled and shook her head.

"Probably not. But then, I don't spend a lot of time outdoors in New York."

"Why not?"

"Too busy with practice."

It sounded lame. She could make time to go to Central Park, or even to the beach. Maybe if she factored more breaks in her schedule she wouldn't feel so overwhelmed and pressured.

She was in control of her life. It was up to her to find the balance.

"It'll work for today," he said, taking her hand again.

Kirk took her to the amphitheater where the music festival would be held later in August. Today there was a rock band playing with lots of teenagers on the stands and sitting on the grass. Many were dancing to the music, others clapped or sang along. He found a spot on the back of the stands and they sat.

"The acoustics are good here," she said.

He nodded. It wasn't bad. He could hear the music and some of the murmur from conversations around them. Usually it was too much effort to listen.

He glanced at Angelica and her new hat. She looked pretty as a picture watching the musicians with an assessing look. He hoped the sunburn would fade and not peel. Though he bet she'd look cute with a peeling nose.

He leaned back against the empty seats behind them, remembering the last time he'd come to the fair. It had been before he'd gone into the army. He'd brought Alice. They'd just graduated from high school and had talked of marriage once he was done with his service. They'd listened to music, rode the rides. He'd even won a silly turtle for her at the pitching booth.

Different experience now with Angelica finding every aspect fascinating. It showed what different upbringing could do. He took it for granted, she was amazed.

If she stayed, after a few years would she take this for granted as well?

He'd never know.

She looked at him and smiled and he felt a kick in the gut. If she had any idea how pretty she was she'd control those smiles.

"You must come every year," she said.

"Nope. First time in a long while."

"Why? This is fabulous."

He sat up.

"It's more fun coming with someone. I didn't have anyone to come with before. Not since Alice."

"No one?"

"No one I wanted to risk gossip enough to bring."

"Is there some rite of passage I don't know about coming here with you?"

"If you were staying, there'd be speculation about our relationship. Bringing someone to the county fair is a pretty strong indication you're involved or thinking about it."

"But not with me?"

"No. You don't live here."

If she did, would he have brought her? If she lived here, he'd have to rethink the entire situation.

But he knew better than to get involved with someone who liked the bright lights and big city. Alice hadn't stayed. He hadn't enough to offer her and she'd told him so in no uncertain terms. There was no reason to think Angelica could ever fit in.

But for today he could pretend. The idea surprised him. The longer he considered it the more he thought, why not? He'd show her around, explain everything to her and enjoy her enthusiasm for the fair.

He hadn't dated anyone seriously since Alice. He was careful not to give the wrong impression to anyone. Or was he guarding his heart against the pain of loss? He wouldn't think about that today.

"Come on, let's hit the carnival section and ride the Ferris wheel," he said, standing and offering his hand again.

A day for just the two of them. Making memories.

As the afternoon progressed, Kirk did his best to give her the best fair experience she'd ever have. And she loved every moment. Laughter was the key word for the day. He hadn't had such fun since before he could remember. During times waiting in line for a ride they talked a bit about their childhoods. So different it was educational in one sense. He still thought she had lacked the carefree days of childhood. And twice she had wistfully told him how lucky he'd been.

When they passed the pitching concession, he offered to try to win her a teddy bear.

"You're kidding?" she said, looking around him to see the stand. Three metal milk bottles stacked pyramid style sat on the back board. A direct hit in only one area would knock all three flying—qualifying for a bear.

He bought some balls. Several other couples stopped to watch, while Angelica stood a few feet away, so not to crowd him.

He threw the first ball which clipped the top bottle. But it only swayed, staying on the other two. His next ball missed completely and everyone laughed. The third ball hit the bottle on the bottom left. Again the bottles swayed, but remained upright.

"I'll take another set of balls," he said.

Now it was getting to crunch time. Several good-natured teasing comments were called. A guy he knew from Bryceville called an insult to his pitching ability—or apparent lack thereof.

"Don't listen to them," Angelica said. "You can do it."

He'd done it before for Alice. He wanted to do it today for Angelica. He threw it for all he was worth. It missed completely. He looked at her and the faith showing in her gaze touched him as nothing had in a long while. She didn't know him, didn't know what he could do, but he could read her confidence in him as if it had been tattooed on her forehead.

He threw the ball and the trio of bottles exploded apart, flying around the concession booth.

"Woohoo!" Angelica said, rushing over to throw her arms around him. "You did it! I knew you could."

The crowd clapped and began drifting away. Kirk's friend called congratulations before moving on.

"Whoa, man, when you connect, you do it in style," the concessioner said, looking at Angelica. "So what color bear do you want?" he asked.

"Pink, please, to match my hat," she said looking over her shoulder.

Kirk liked the feel of her in his arms. Giving her a hug, he slowly released her so she could take the big pink teddy bear. Grinning, she looked at him.

"Thank you, no one has ever won a teddy bear for me before."

"My pleasure."

The feel of her soft body against his felt imprinted. She walked along beside him and all he could think of was to find a place to pull her back into his arms to kiss her.

Twilight was fading into darkness when Kirk drove into the driveway of Webb Francis's home. Angelica held the bear with one arm, the other encircling him as the motorcycle rode through the quiet evening. Her hat had been squashed between them so it wouldn't blow away.

"That was the best day ever," she said when they stopped.

Slowly she withdrew her hand when he turned to help her off the bike. He scooped up her pink hat and pushed it back into shape while she removed the helmet.

He took it, the bike still rumbling.

"Thank you," she said, leaning over to kiss him.

He pulled her closer, relishing the taste of her, the feel of her in his arms. The kiss was awkward with him still straddling the bike, but he wouldn't have changed a second of it. When she straightened, he released her. He tried to gauge her expression in the dim light but it was impossible. All he could see was wide eyes and a stunned expression.

"I'll see you in," he said.

"Not necessary. It's only a few steps. Thanks again. I had a fabulous time."

She seemed to run away. He watched until she was inside and the light went on in the kitchen. He was hot after that kiss. And she'd participated as much as he did. Yet she'd skittered away like a fawn startled beyond expectations.

He frowned, studying the dark door. Putting together all she'd said about her past, was it possible in this day and age she had never had a serious relationship with a guy? No, that'd be impossible. She was too pretty, too talented.

She lived in New York City, for heaven's sake.

Slowly he backed the bike until he could turn around. Driving the short distance to his driveway, he tried to argue the situation, but the more he thought about it, the more he grew certain she was a novice in the dating scene.

"Oh, no," he groaned when he shut down the bike and propped it on its stand. That would change everything.

Surprisingly, he'd had a fabulous day, too.

Which raised red flags all over the place.

He could not fall for the pretty violinist from New York. She was leaving, as all the women in his life had left. At least he knew ahead of time that this relationship had no future. He hoped he was wise enough to guard his heart or he'd be head over heels before he knew it.

His family had bad luck when it came to women. Did the men choose unwisely? Or were circumstances stacked against them?

He went to get a cold drink, then headed to the studio. Restless, too keyed up to sleep, he wanted to escape his thoughts. He needed to focus on the carving and not the unattainable woman next door. She'd be gone soon. He just had to wait her out.

Angelica was about to turn off the light and head upstairs to read before bed when the phone rang. It was Professor Simmons.

"Sorry to be calling so late. I've tried several times during the day. How are you doing there?" he asked.

"I'm having a great time. Sorry I wasn't here when you called. Actually, I was at a county fair." She smiled, remembering the many ways of entertainment she'd seen that day.

"Well, that sounds different."

"It was so much fun. We rode carnival rides like kids. The

man who took me won me a teddy bear, and we ate so much I might not eat again for a week. Did you know cotton candy just melts in your mouth?"

"Ah, don't believe I've ever had cotton candy."

She shook her head. This was one of her former professors. Serious, focused. She must sound like an idiot to him.

"Are you doing okay there on your own? I didn't know Webb Francis was sick when I suggested you look him up," Professor Simmons continued.

"I'm doing better than fine. He's letting me stay here in his place. Well, you had to know that or you wouldn't have called here. He has a fantastic collection of folk music. And I'm even teaching two young kids how to play the fiddle."

"The fiddle?" he repeated.

She laughed.

"I'm getting used to calling it that. Everyone looks a bit blank when I call it a violin. I'm able to pick up a lot of the songs merely by listening. And Webb Francis has a ton of sheet music."

"You have a rare gift of hearing and playing without music. So are you glad you went?"

"Oh, I love it here. We listened to different musical groups at the fair. There'll be even more at the music festival, I understand. That's at the end of August. It's amazing to watch the people really get into the music, clapping, sometimes singing along. I wouldn't have missed this opportunity for anything. Thank you for your recommendation."

"I'm pleased it's turning out well. Actually, I called because your parents called me two days ago wanting to know if I had the phone number of the place you were staying, as your cell wasn't working. I said there was no cell service I knew of in Smoky Hollow. From the questions that followed, I realized you hadn't told them where you were going. I hope I didn't mess things up telling them where you were."

"Oops. Sorry, Professor Simmons. This vacation was supposed to be a break from everything, not just the symphony."

"You might give them a call. They sounded worried."

"Thanks for letting me know. I didn't mean to put you in the middle of anything."

"Sometimes families exert pressures that are not fully realized at the time. I know they were strongly supportive of your music when you were a student here."

"Maybe too much. I'm grown up now. I can make my own decisions. Did you ever consider delving more into folk music?"

"I have on occasion. Teaching that course gives me an outlet that combines my love for it with other duties at the school. I have spent several summers in Smoky Hollow with Webb Francis. He has a rare talent himself. And knows more about that kind of music than anyone. You'll have a good teacher, once he's well again."

"Did you ever go to the music festival the end of August?"

"Of course. You'll not want to miss that. There will be jug bands, dulcimers and real old-fashioned mountain folk music. Great songs handed down from the first settlers. Call me when you return to New York. You can tell me all about your experiences in Kentucky."

"I'll do that. Thanks for everything, Professor."

She hung up feeling guilty that she had put him in an awkward position. But she'd never expected her parents to call him to find out where she was. Had they called everyone she knew until they reached him? Couldn't they give her a few weeks on her own?

Reluctantly, she picked up the phone and dialed home. The phone rang until the answering machine picked up.

114 | BARBARA MCMAHON

"Hi Mom, it's Angelica. I, um, was just calling to say hi. I'll call back."

She reluctantly gave them the phone number. She didn't want them calling her every day trying to talk her into returning to New York. But she could understand they wanted to be in touch. Sorry to say, she hadn't missed their presence in her life at all since she'd been in Smoky Hollow. She had a freedom she'd never known before and she relished every moment.

Still, this was the longest she'd been out of touch with her parents. Gazing out the window she wondered why it had taken her so long to break free. She didn't need nor want her parents dictating her every move. She was totally capable. From now on, she'd dictate her own destiny.

Angelica knew they only wanted what was best for her. Older when she'd been born, they had given up on having any children. So it was a double whammy—doting older parents and gifted child.

Restless, she changed her mind about going up to bed and went to practice the song she was planning to play in the festival. It was complex enough to keep her fully engaged while playing, forcing out all worries and thoughts of the future. There was only the bow, the strings and the fast pace to the music.

After an hour, she put down the violin. She was getting better all the time, but would anyone really care?

She walked over to the window to look at Kirk's house, remembering his kiss at the end of their date. She'd had such fun that day. The Ferris wheel had given them an aerial view of the fairgrounds. The different music had enforced her decision to get more variety into her musical repertoire. And she couldn't wait to have cotton candy again.

Yet who knew the touch of two lips could set off a firestorm?

And she hadn't a clue what to do about it. On the one hand, she wanted more. To see if every time he kissed her she about melted in desire. Or would she grow used to them? Would they lose their magical touch?

No lights showed at his house. He must have gone to bed. Which she should do. Then she saw the lights on in the building behind his house. Giving in to impulse, she went to see what he was doing.

The door to the building stood open, spilling light in a wide path. Angelica stopped in the opening and stared at the workshop. It was definitely not a garage. There were wooden statues and figurines against one wall. Piled up in front of another wall were chunks of wood in various sizes. In the center Kirk was chiseling from a huge block of raw wood. She glanced at what he was doing but her attention was immediately drawn to the glowing statue of a mother and children toward the back. Slowly she walked in and over to the wooden piece.

"This is amazing," she said reaching out to gently touched the wood.

He swung around.

"What are you doing here?"

"This is your whittling? What an understatement. It's amazing." She marveled at the satin finish so smooth beneath her fingertips.

She knew he watched her. When she looked up, she met his gaze.

"These are beautiful."

"Thanks."

She walked along the finished pieces, reaching out to touch, unable to help herself. The rich colors in the wood, the tones and shadows and highlights were startling in their clarity and highlighted the skill of the carver for each piece. Time and again she was drawn back to the mother-and-children piece.

"Will this be sold in an art gallery?" she asked.

"Hope so. I have contacts to several across the South."

"This is how you make your living, not construction or whittling. These are amazing."

She walked over to the piece he was working on.

"What's this going to be?"

"Woman on the precipice," he said.

She could see the vague shape already chiseled from the wood. A bluff, a bank of trees growing back from the edge and on the edge the figure that was rough cut at best.

"Can I watch you work?" she asked, fascinated by the amazing talent he had. She'd never suspected.

"Pretty boring. I shave small bits off, see how it looks, do more," he said, looking back at the work in progress.

"How long will this take to finish?"

She walked around it looking at it from all angles. She wouldn't have the first clue on how to do something like this. She looked at Kirk. He looked back, the same man who had teased her at the fair, had shared corn dogs and held her on the Ferris wheel when he'd rocked the car causing her to squeal in mock alarm.

Her heart caught in her throat. The same man who had confused her more than anyone with their goodbye kiss earlier.

"Several weeks," he said.

Angelica looked around and spotted a stool. She brought it closer and sat on it.

"Ignore me."

She kept her eyes on the wood, hoping he'd let her stay. She was fascinated this virile man did such delicate work. Glancing at the mother again she noted the serene look about the face, even without minute details. It could be any mother. Perhaps that added to the appeal.

She couldn't wait to see how he finished this piece.

Once he started it was obvious he could ignore her and focus on the work. She watched him, fascinated as his large hands did such precision work. The tools looked tiny, the gouging and chiseling precise and controlled. His hands were scarred. She thought from construction. Now she knew it was more likely from slips from the chisel or other tools. The patience and care he took removing bits of wood seemed ageless. If she were doing it, she'd rush through to completion. But it wouldn't be as amazing as Kirk's art pieces were.

The only sound was the soft tap of the hammer against the chisel. He changed to a gouge, worked some with that. Then took a piece of sandpaper and rubbed lightly, studying the area from several different angles. She could almost see the tree take shape, the detail on the leaves and branches startling. If he did that with each tree blocked out, no wonder it took weeks to complete. But it'd be exquisite when finished.

"Where did you get the idea?" she asked.

He glanced at her.

"From you."

"Me?" Angelica frowned. "I've never stood on the edge of a cliff."

"You're on one right now, if you think about it. Behind you is the forest of your past. Ahead, nothing familiar, nothing normal. You're poised on the brink. Will you take a step out in faith and change your life? Or will you hesitate, then turn and reenter the forest of familiar?"

She stared at it a long moment.

"What do you think?" she asked.

Could she step out and find new fulfillment in life? Or was she destined to stay on the path her parents had laid out?

"You have accomplished great things for a woman your age. I think you'll go back to the familiar."

She wasn't sure if she liked that idea or not.

On the other hand, this was a graphic example of what could happen if she went forward—there would be a drop and splat and she'd be done.

Kirk wondered what she'd say to his assessment. Came from years of experience. There were only a few hearty souls who found the happiness in life in this small town. Those who farmed the land and passed it down from generation to generation, like Ben and Carrie. Or those who had seen what the rest of the world had to offer and selected this town, like he had and Webb Francis.

He didn't judge her. He wanted her to be happy and suspected the familiar route was the best way for her to go. This visit was merely a slight detour in her life's road. One she might remember for years, but wouldn't significantly alter anything.

"Were you ever on a precipice?" she asked.

"Sure, everyone goes through that stage, don't you think?"

He picked up a wide flat blade and worked some on the cliff. It could be chunky to offer a way down and onward. It should be smooth in some areas to show the unknown, the possible danger of a sheer fall.

"And what did you choose?" she asked.

"Not the familiar or I'd be a farmer like my granddad. But enough of the familiar to settle in the town I grew up in. To build a community. To know my neighbors and friends."

"Yet you touch the outside world with your art," she said.

"I'm not a hermit. I travel sometimes. But I'm always glad to return home. I've seen things I wished I hadn't when I was in the army. Been places no one else in town has been after that. And seen sights like no others where it grabs you by the throat and make you thank God for the opportunity to see one of His wonders."

"Yet you come back here."

"Time and again," he said, nodding.

"Alice wanted more. Does that mean you want less?" she asked.

He stopped working, putting down his tools.

"How is it wanting less to be happy here?"

"I don't know. All my life I've heard go to New York, make it big."

"And are you happy?"

She thought a moment, then slowly shook her head.

"You know that. It's why I'm here, trying to learn something new, see what else is out there."

He reached for her and drew her to her feet, folding her into his arms.

"Do you have a special male friend, Angel?"

She shook her head, her eyes unable to look away. Her heart raced. Her fingers grabbed hold of his shirt, feeling the warmth from his chest, the heat from his eyes.

"People who are happy here have someone special in their lives. They are building family. Connecting with neighbors and finding satisfaction in the work they do and the leisure activities they choose."

She swallowed, feeling inept and unsure.

"Have you ever had a special male friend?" he asked softly, resting his forehead on hers.

All she could see was Kirk's dark eyes, gazing deeply into hers.

Slowly she shook her head, moving both of them. She felt surrounded by heat, rising desire, wishing he'd stop talking and kiss her. It was scary and thrilling. For this moment, she did feel on the edge of a precipice. Would his kiss send her soaring or have her fall flat on her face?

So slowly she thought she'd never stand it, he lifted his face then leaned closer, giving her time to pull away if that was what she wanted. Then he closed his eyes and kissed her.

Angelica closed her eyes and savored every aspect of the kiss, from the warm lips moving against hers, to the hard body cradling her, to the sensations that blotted out everything else but the two of them.

The sensations were pure delight. She felt she was soaring. His lips moved again, teasing responses she didn't know she could give. When he deepened the kiss, she clung, excitement swirling through her. She'd never felt this mixture of exquisite delight and yearning desire for more. She pressed closer, wishing she could become part of Kirk, meld the two of them until they were one. Reveling in the kiss, hoping it'd never end, she gave herself up to the moment.

When his mouth left hers to trail kisses across her cheeks, her arms moved to encircle his neck. She could feel the hard muscles of his chest against her breasts. She could feel the long length of him bent to accommodate her shorter stature. Mostly she felt the trailing fire and ice his hands brought, pressing her closer, closer.

He kissed her mouth again and again, kisses that inflamed her. The temperature rose several degrees as the heat they generated could have warmed a winter's day.

A moment later he rested his forehead against hers again. Slowly she opened her eyes, almost drowning in the deep chocolate brown of his. Her heart raced, her skin tingled, her soul soared.

"You're one dangerous woman," he said softly.

Her knees were weak, her body lethargic. All she wanted to do was kiss him again and again. See where that might lead—as if she didn't know.

"Go home, Angel. Go to Webb Francis's house tonight and back to New York tomorrow. This isn't your place."

Chapter Eight

If he'd dumped a bucket of cold water over her he couldn't have shocked her more. After kisses like that, he wanted her to leave?

She pulled away and walked across to the door, trying to get control of her emotions. Disappointment and frustration warred with anger and pride. She couldn't think. If she had a talent for words, she'd come up with some snappy reply that would put him in the same anguish she felt. Nothing came to mind, only the echo of his words. Go home. This is not your place.

Go away from me, he might as well have shouted the words. She thought she might be falling in love with this complex mysterious man and he wanted her gone. How could she have read the signs so wrong?

At the door she finally had enough courage to turn and glare at him.

"I'm here until after the festival. I won't burden you with my presence again. But I'm not leaving until I'm good and ready. So deal with it."

Once clear of the door, she ran across the lawn, hoping she wouldn't stumble and fall on her face in the darkness. She ran up the steps and into the cottage, shutting the door just before tears welled in her eyes. She refused to cry over the man. She hardly knew him. She'd met him a short time ago. Never mind the feelings he engendered in her. He'd made his point very clear.

Way to go, Devon, Kirk thought as he watched her leave.

But it was being proactive or succumb to the siren call she gave without even knowing it. He'd thought he'd fallen in love once, lost the woman to a way of life he didn't want.

In retrospect, he wondered how much he'd loved Alice. Had it been companionship, friendship that had moved beyond high school? If he'd really loved her above all else, he'd have moved to Atlanta. If he'd offered her all she needed, she'd have insisted they stay together.

He knew better than to take up with a woman who came from a different world. He liked living in Smoky Hollow. He liked his work, liked helping out, liked being with friends he'd known his entire life. Traveling when the mood struck, working on construction when needed, being near his crusty grandfather all made his life the way he wanted it.

Clenching his fists, he looked around the studio. Would he ever see it again without picturing her sitting so still watching him in fascination as he carved? Without remembering the intoxication of her kisses, the feminine feel of her body, the fire that had swept through him with her pressed against him?

He didn't want to have feelings for Angelica. She'd leave—just like every other woman in his life. The men in his family just weren't enough to keep women with them. His mother had wanted more. Alice had wanted more. How soon before Angelica knew he wasn't enough for her and wanted more? Better to make a clean cut now than drag out the hope for her to stay when he knew that would be impossible.

He hoped he hadn't wrecked his future peace of mind by giving in to temptation and kissing her until he scarcely remembered his own name. He took a deep breath, still smelling the fragrance of her unique scent. He closed his eyes, still feeling the imprint of her soft curves against his harder frame. Hearing the catch in her breathing when she discovered the passion that he suspected she'd never tapped before.

She was some innocent young woman who should be wined and dined by men of her own background. Taken to restaurants and the theater in New York, not some country fair and music festival.

Snapping open his eyes, he moved to the carving. The sooner he set to forgetting Angelica Cannon, the better he'd be.

He'd been cruel to protect himself. She was dabbling in a way of life vastly different from her own. She was not contemplating a move to Smoky Hollow, she'd said over and over she was returning to New York at the end of August. He had less than a month to get through. A month to ignore the next-door neighbor and concentrate on the sculpture.

The sculpture of her.

No matter how he tried to pretend it was anyone else, he'd admitted the truth. This was her. When he carved the face, it would be Angel's. When he thought about the symbolism, it'd be of her life, her summer in Kentucky.

Could he capture the yearning for something new mixed with the fate of returning to the familiar? Could he make the impossible decision clear on a face that would be scarcely four inch high?

Could he, and not wish for a different outcome every second he worked on it?

Disgusted with his own thoughts, he turned off the light and closed the door. He'd get something to eat and then get to bed at a halfway reasonable hour.

If she stayed away, this infatuation would fade within days.

He'd start tomorrow by visiting Webb Francis before he was discharged, and then spending the rest of the day in Bryceville. Time apart would be best. It was less than four weeks.

The next morning Kirk rose early and went to see his grandfather before heading to Bryceville. Visiting hours at the hospital didn't start until ten, so he might as well see what he could help out with at the farm before going to see Webb Francis.

It was barely dawn when he pulled into the farmyard. Lights were on in the kitchen, and he knew he'd be in time for breakfast. Beat eating alone this morning.

"I didn't expect to see you," his grandfather said when he entered.

"I'm going to Bryceville later. So I thought I'd swing by here and see what you needed before I left."

"Seeing Webb Francis?"

"He's supposed to be discharged tomorrow. I wanted to catch him before he goes to Betsy's."

Once breakfast was on the table Hiram looked at Kirk.

"Where's that New York gal this morning?"

"Home, I guess."

"She seemed a nice enough woman."

Kirk nodded. He'd come here to escape thoughts of Angelica, he didn't want a discussion with his grandfather about her.

"Have you heard her play?"

"No. But according to Webb Francis, she must be good. I told you she's working with a couple of kids from town. Sam plans to play in the festival. Angelica does, too."

"Ummm."

"Do you want to go this year?"

Kirk knew his grandfather didn't attend the music festivals and hadn't in two decades, no matter how much Webb Francis and others pressed him to attend.

"Might."

Kirk looked at him.

"Say again?"

"I said I might go. Why look so surprised, I used to go all the time."

"True. Are you going to sing?"

"Nope. But I might go to hear that gal play. If she's so good, it might be worth hearing. Listen to her play sometime and tell me."

"Ask her to play for you," Kirk said.

His plan was to avoid Angelica as much as possible. He didn't want to get deeper involved.

Even though, for a split second, he welcomed the suggestion as a way to see her again. Not for himself, but for his grandfather.

"She's staying next door to you, be neighborly and go listen to her play."

Coming to breakfast had been a mistake. Now he either had to sound like an idiot with his reasons for not wanting to listen to her play, or go and be caught up in that fascinated attraction.

"I'm going to replace the back fence around the hog pen soon. Some of the boards are getting too splintered to hold up. Don't want them fool hogs out roaming the countryside," Hiram said.

Kirk nodded, glad the topic of conversation changed.

"I'll give you a hand. When were you thinking?"

"Next week? Maybe."

"Want me to pick up the wood?"

The two of them discussed the project and once breakfast was over went out to the fence to determine what to replace and how long it might take.

It was midafternoon by the time Kirk drove into his driveway. He'd had a good visit with Webb Francis and done some shopping in Bryceville. He'd also run by the lumber yard and ordered the wood to repair the fence. He'd pick it up next week.

Once again he noticed the ragged lawn in front of Webb Francis's house. His own could use a cutting as well. It was hot, but not that hot.

He changed into old clothes, drank a couple of glasses of water and then went to mow his and his neighbor's lawn.

Having mowed his lawn a couple of weeks ago, it was easy enough to get it taken care of. Webb Francis's was another matter. The tall grass took more effort to mow. He made a dozen or so passes across the width of the lawn and grew hotter with each step. Some of the yard was in shade, but most was in full sun this time of day.

He stripped off his shirt and tossed it onto a bush, pushing the old power mower back and forth. At this rate, it'd be dark before he finished. He should have tackled it earlier.

Sam and Teresa Ann came onto the porch, followed by Angelica. Kirk caught sight of them and waved, not pausing in his task.

The kids each had a glass in hand watching him as they drank. He could use a glass of iced tea right about now. But didn't want to stop work to go make some. One-third down, another two-thirds to go. If he didn't finish now, he'd have to plan on it tomorrow. Cutting grass wasn't his favorite activity. Might as well finish now.

He made two more passes then was startled to see Angelica walking to him a large glass of amber liquid in hand.

"If that's iced tea, I'll—"

He stopped suddenly remembering what kissing her caused.

He reached for the glass. Heavenly. He drank it all without stopping.

"Hot work," she said.

At least that's what he thought she said. It was harder to hear over the roar of the lawn mower.

"Do you want more?" she asked.

"Please. Appreciate it."

He watched her walk back to the house, speak to the children, and then go inside. Minutes later she was walking across the lawn. He'd done another half swath. She handed him the glass when he stopped.

"I probably should be doing that, I'm staying in Webb Francis's house," she said, eyeing the lawn mower with some trepidation.

"Have a shot," he said, stepping back.

He didn't know if he wanted to drink the tea or pour it over his body. Being near her wasn't cooling him down.

She met his eyes and nodded.

"Okay. Just push it?"

He nodded. "Never mowed a lawn before?"

She shook her head as she gripped the handle and pushed. For a second nothing happened, then with a bit more pressure, the lawn mower began to move, spitting out the cut grass as she tried to follow the edge of his last cut. When clumps of tall grass appeared between her path and his, he knew she found it tougher than anticipated. It would have been easier if the grass was shorter to start with. Sipping the tea, he watched her, grinning at the effort—and the missed spots.

Angelica pushed harder. This wasn't as easy as Kirk made it seem. Finally reaching the edge, she struggled to turn it back. Viewing what she'd cut, she was dismayed to see spots where the machine hadn't cut straight. There were patches looking like a Mohawk along the edge between Kirk's cut and her own. Determined to do better, she pushed again, getting the machine going. It wasn't as hard to keep it going as to start. Still when she reached him, she was burning up with heat—not all attributed to the effort to push the lawn mower.

He handed her the glass and took over without a word. Stepping to one side, she watched him. The muscles contracted when he pushed. Sculpted, they testified to the strength of the man. Working in construction and carving huge pieces of wood required strength. She was fascinated. Wishing she could touch him, she blinked and looked at the house. The two children were watching. She smiled and walked to the porch. He'd made it abundantly clear he wanted nothing to do with her. She needed to remember that.

"You didn't do so good, Miss Cannon," Sam said.

She could depend on that child for total honesty.

"It was my first time. I think cutting grass requires practice, like playing the fiddle, don't you?"

"I guess."

"My daddy says cutting grass is man's work. Then Mama takes him iced tea just like you did, Miss Cannon," Teresa Ann said. "Only they end up kissing and all."

"Ew, gross," Sam said.

Angelica looked back at Kirk. She wouldn't have minded a kiss for her effort. Or one to reward him for his work.

But after yesterday, she was firmly squelching any thoughts in that direction. It was too bad her body didn't listen to her mind. Her fingers tingled with the desire to touch him. Her mouth yearned for the feel of his. Her heart raced, and not from the effort to propel that machine.

"Thank you for the limonade."

Teresa Ann handed Angelica her empty glass.

"Tomorrow I won't be here for practice, we're going to the fair. But I could come on Saturday."

"If you want. I'll be here."

"Me, too. I want to make sure I'm ready for the festival," Sam said.

"Okay, then, Saturday it is."

She watched them run off, wondering how they found the energy in this heat. She took the glasses inside and put them in the sink. Giving in to temptation, she went back to the screen door to watch Kirk. She didn't think he could see her. She hoped he couldn't.

How pathetic to be caught staring at the most virile man she knew when he'd told her to go home. He was so not feeling the same attraction she was.

When he finally finished, she realized she'd been watching for almost an hour. Stepping away, she went to rinse out the glasses and then went to the music room. It took two seconds to tidy it up after the children's lesson. Picking up her violin, she began her own practice. She wanted to play this song for the festival and it was trickier than originally thought.

She was on her second pass when she caught movement from the corner of her eye. Stopping, she looked at the doorway. Kirk stood there watching her.

"I knocked, but you couldn't hear me, I guess," he said.

"What can I do for you?"

She tried to keep her eyes firmly on his and not drop her gaze to the tantalizing expanse of tanned chest that showed off his pecs so well. He held his shirt in one hand. His jeans were riding low, which made her gulp and become desperate not to let her glance waver from his dark eyes.

"I heard you playing, wanted to hear more. Orange Blossom Special, isn't it?"

She nodded.

"Hard piece to play, so I've heard."

"You've heard right. I'm determined, however," she said.

"Sounds good. I'll let my granddad know."

"Why would he care?"

"He's planning to come to the festival this year. First time in two decades. He wants to hear you play. He said if Webb Francis thought you were good, maybe you are."

She laughed. "So he wants to verify that himself?"

"I reckon he does."

"I still want to go back to his farm and hear him sing that song. I found the music and have been practicing that one as well."

"I expect he'll be pleased to hear that."

The phone sounded.

"Who would that be?" she asked, putting down the violin and heading toward the kitchen. Kirk moved out of her way, then followed.

"Mother!"

Angelica was startled to hear her mother on the other end of the line. She'd hoped to have more time before having to talk to her.

"What in the world are you doing in the backwoods of Appalachia, Angelica?" her mother demanded. "I can't believe you took off and never said a word. What were you thinking?"

"I'm taking a vacation," she said.

Guilt infiltrated. She tried to rationalize she had the right, but old habits were hard to break.

Kirk stepped closer and watched her. He couldn't hear the other side of the conversation, but she knew he could hear her.

"And you just take off without a word to your father and me? I can't believe you left so abruptly and didn't contact us."

She was staring at Kirk's bare chest, bronzed by the sun, defined by muscles from his work. None of the men she knew looked so good.

"Angelica!"

"What do you want me to say? I wanted to take a vacation, so I did. I'm entitled."

She turned halfway away from Kirk to better focus on her mother's tirade.

"Well, of course you can take a vacation. You should have told us, we would have rented a cottage at the Cape."

"I didn't want to go to Cape Cod this year. I wanted a total break and a chance to explore different music. I decided to come here."

"Now is the time to be scheduling future concerts, renewing your contract with the philharmonic, not hiding away in the woods. Good grief, what were you thinking? You have to keep constantly in the public's eye to build a following. Which is the reason I'm calling. Your agent has a marvelous opportunity for you in Europe. For two months, you'd tour some of the capitals, Paris, Rome, Madrid, Berlin. It's a fantastic chance to build recognition abroad as well as enhance your CV here in the states."

"As a soloist?" Angelica asked, feeling things closing in on her.

She didn't want to have to do a tour in Europe. She wanted to stay right here. The thought startled her and she looked at Kirk. He was watching her with the intensity she'd grown used to.

"Yes. Call him today. He's been calling us for days, frantic to get in touch with you."

"I'll call later."

"Now, Angelica."

Angelica gripped the phone. She'd left New York to escape the pressure of her life. Her mother was jumping in with both feet and she resented it.

This was her life, not her mother's.

"You're needed back in New York."

"I'll call later," she said, infusing her voice with determination.

This was her first vacation ever. She discounted family outings to the Cape. She was not going to cut it short.

"I can't believe I'm hearing this. You have had the best musical education money can buy. And you choose to go to some backwoods area in Kentucky for your vacation? And now you're delaying calling your agent. What has come over you?"

"This is what I want for this summer," she tried to explain.

Already she was feeling the pressure to conform to their plan for her future. They couldn't understand her desire to break away and learn more than just the classics and modern music. She wanted—

"There was a great program at the Cape this summer. You should have gone there. At least you'd have been closer to home," her mother said. "And more available when your agent called. I can't believe you aren't jumping at the chance for this tour. It's amazing, and to be offered to one so young is simply miraculous. You need to grasp the chance, these don't come along all the time."

Angelica glanced at Kirk. He was staring intently at her and she wondered how much he could hear. He looked at her quizzically.

Frustration rose.

"Mom, I'll take care of it."

She knew her voice was rising, but she was angry her mother kept harping on this when Angelica had been enjoying her break from routine. She was not a child.

Kirk placed his hand over hers holding the phone and pulled it away. "What?" he asked softly.

"She won't listen."

"Then hang up," he said.

She stared at him. Then put the phone back to her ear. Her mother was talking, but she'd missed most of what she'd said.

"I have to go now, Mom. Goodbye."

Then she hung up the phone. Staring at it in amazement, she couldn't believe she'd hung up on her mother.

"Angelica," he said.

She looked up.

"You've done nothing wrong. You're a capable adult, fully able to make your own decisions. Why get upset over a conversation on the phone?"

"They act like I can't think for myself. Like I have to fulfil some great scheme to be the best violinist ever in the world. And before this summer, I've always let them tell me what to do. I'm not sure I can stand up to them."

"Just say no," he said.

She repeated the phrase and nodded.

"Here's hoping."

The phone rang again. Angelica looked at it and then shrugged.

"Let it ring. Thanks for cutting the grass. It smells so fresh. And the roses show better without the scraggly grass. Want more tea?"

The phone continued to ring.

"Let's move to the porch," she suggested.

She'd never deliberately ignored her parents in her life. It felt oddly liberating. She was an adult. She could make her own choices. And right now she chose to not answer the phone just because it was ringing.

After Kirk had left, however, Angelica began to feel a twinge of guilt. She should at least see what her agent had to say. She could always just say no.

Calling him, she was surprised how anxious he was to speak to her.

"Never leave town without leaving a forwarding phone number," he said.

"I'm on vacation," she said, not at all pressured by Henry, not like with her parents. "My mother said you have a gig?"

"I cringe at your slang. This is a marvelous opportunity to showcase your best work in a tour of five capitals in Europe, several concerts in each venue. It's in conjunction with the Musique Francais production. How can you refuse?"

"When and where?" she asked.

The Musique Francais was very prestigious. Her mother was right, this would be the opportunity of a lifetime—especially for one as young as she was.

"Rome, Berlin, Madrid, Paris and London. Starting the second week in September. I've already stalled longer than I should have, trying to reach you. You'd have to fly to London to begin rehearsals and practice next week. There is no time to waste. How soon can you be back in New York?"

"That's a problem," Angelica said. "I'm teaching two students and can't leave before the music festival."

"What? You're teaching!" Henry sounded astonished. "That's preposterous. Unless—are they gifted—would I need to hear them?"

"They're learning folk songs from this area, so I don't think they are your average client, Henry. Actually it's turning out to be quite fun. I love the excitement they have for learning. And I'm learning as much by helping them. I did promise I'd do what I could to get Sam ready for the festival. He's worked so hard. They plan to come practice even on a Saturday. How's that for dedication?"

"Whatever are you thinking?" he asked. "You aren't a teacher—you're a gifted violinist."

Angelica explained, ending with, "So, you see, I have to meet this commitment."

"I see nothing of the sort. The child is eight. He can practice on his own. Let the locals teach him. Let him wing it. You're needed here and then in Europe."

"There's no teacher until Webb Francis gets well. And I made a commitment."

"Break it. This is far more important. Do you know how rare it is to get this kind of chance?"

She bit her lip with indecision. She did know how rare it was. And what a boost to her career it'd be to have this to include in her CV.

Then Sam's face danced before her. He was counting on her.

"I'll have to let you know."

"Angelica."

"I'll think about it and call you back in a day or so. Goodbye."

She was getting good at ending conversations when she was finished being harangued by the other party. At least he didn't have her phone number to keep calling like her mother did.

She went to sit on the porch, gazing at the newly mowed lawn, feeling the heat seep into her. For an instant she felt like a reprimanded schoolgirl. Taking a breath, she hoped she could focus on the decision needed and not her frustration with the way others treated her. She appreciated the work Henry did for her. But ultimately, it was her decision in which way to take her career.

The thought of playing in some of the capitals of Europe was very tempting. A few weeks ago she'd have jumped at the chance. Now, she wanted to take a little time and consider all the ramifications. Maybe a walk would clear her head. She headed toward town and the familiar sights there.

Melvin and Paul were on the porch and she waved, but didn't stop. Only when she was getting uncomfortably hot did she retrace her steps.

Mentally listing all the positive aspects of her vacation, she wanted to be able to articulate all her reasons if she decided against this tour. She didn't touch on the one where she felt smothered and confined with the direction her parents so supported. Somehow she had to come up with a logical reason not to take the tour or accept and give up the vacation she was enjoying.

Kirk knocked on her door just before six pm. He'd showered and changed and looked amazing in a blue cotton shirt and khaki pants. She let him in and stepped back lest she give in to the overwhelming temptation to throw herself into his arms.

"What's up?" she asked.

"I thought you might like to get away for a while. We could eat at the diner."

She studied him for a moment, wondering about his earlier ultimatum to get out of town. She didn't know what had changed, but smiled and nodded.

"I'd love it. I've been with too many spinning thoughts this afternoon."

"How old did you say you were?"

"I know, my parents can be bit overbearing. This is the first time I've challenged them with anything and I think they don't know how to handle it. I'm their only child, I've been so dutiful all along, this is a major change. My mother wanted me to spend the summer at Cape Cod. My father usually goes along with what my mother wants."

"Most kids rebel sometime in their teens. This is hardly rebellion in a major sense, but maybe you're overdue. And I can't see how what you do impacts their lives now that you're grown and on your own. You live in Manhattan, not Boston."

Ruefully she shrugged.

"I'm sure it's better to say my daughter is touring Europe than she's in the boonies of Kentucky."

"They're snobs," he said easily.

Angelica wanted to refute that. She even opened her mouth, then shut it. Thinking about it, were her parents snobs?

"You could be right. I never thought about it before."

He tapped his finger against her chin.

"You're a bit of a snob yourself."

"I am not."

"Not so much now, but I remember your look of horror when you stepped off the bus."

"It wasn't snobbery, it was astonishment that I was still in America and stepped off into such a different world."

She didn't know whether to be insulted or not. She didn't want to be thought of as a snob.

"Ready to go? I thought we could take the bike."

She grinned.

"Snobs do not ride motorcycles."

"So maybe you're broadening your horizons," he said.

He got on the bike and waited. Angelica put her helmet on, wishing she and Kirk could just drive away and keep going until they ran out of gas. Evade making any decisions, just go where the mood struck.

She wanted to defend her choices, share with her parents her delight in the friendly people in Smoky Hollow who had gone out of their way to make her welcome. Convey all the new experiences that flooded her every day. The fun she was having.

When they sat in the booth at the diner Angelica realized how out of place her parents would be in a setting like this.

Their sophisticated clothing would shout to the world they were not from Smoky Hollow. She knew her mother would look with disdain at Angelica's appearance. She'd worn nice slacks and a cotton top—perfectly suited to the community. She liked the feeling of fitting in. Her mother would be critical.

She refused to let her mother's voice echo in her mind. She wondered when she'd felt that way before—if ever. Glancing at Kirk, she made a decision–no more dwelling on what others thought. This was her vacation and she'd spend it however she wanted.

Chapter Nine

Kirk sat back as far as the bench seat allowed once he'd ordered, watching Angelica study the menu. He knew she wasn't seeing the words as her eyes never moved. She was lost in thought. He waited another minute.

"You okay?" he asked.

She looked up and nodded. Laying the menu down, she sighed softly.

"It always gets complicated when dealing with my parents."

"You don't have to deal with them here. They're a thousand miles away."

She shrugged.

"Look at it as you've made a commitment and you need to follow through. Aren't they big on complying with commitments?" he said softly.

"Of course, but usually the commitments are ones they've chosen."

"I don't think Sam Tanner and Teresa Ann Williams care who chose the commitment, they're counting on you to help them. Sam plans to play in the festival for the first time. He's eight. Not a bad thing for a kid that young. Would you end that dream?"

"If Webb Francis recovers soon enough, he can handle things."

"It'll be luck if he's back by the time the festival starts. He won't be back in time to help Sam. Plus, I'm looking forward to hearing you play Orange Blossom Special."

She smiled. "You might not be so glad once you've heard me. It's tricky."

"Most of us in Smoky Hollow will never get to New York to hear the philharmonic. You wouldn't deny us the chance to hear you this summer, would you? It's not as if you're planning to stay here the rest of your life."

He knew he kept repeating that as if it were a mantra. Maybe he'd believe it one day.

Even if she did stay, *which she wouldn't*, he had nothing to offer. The residents of Smoky Hollow chose their lifestyle for the most part. They didn't get into it by default. Webb Francis had done his stint in New York and San Francisco, and except for himself, was probably the most traveled of anyone in town. But they weren't the only ones who had traveled and seen the world.

When the food came, Angelica relaxed a little commenting on how delicious the pot roast she'd ordered tasted. Gradually he could feel the tension slip away. Not wanting to risk a return, Kirk tried to keep the conversation into noncontroversial topics.

"I appreciate your asking me to dinner," she said when they both finished. "I don't know what I'm going to do."

"About?"

She studied him a moment then said, "My agent has a fantastic opportunity to do a tour in Europe in the fall. Six months ago I would have jumped at the chance with no hesitation. Now— I don't know."

He dropped his gaze to the last of the iced tea in his glass. Another reason she'd never fit into his niche. She was a world-class concert violinist, with the opportunity to tour Europe. He looked out the window at the empty street, the trees that crowded nearby. Nothing like the capitals of Europe. Nothing he had or could offer would ever compete.

"What are you going to do?" he asked.

"I have no idea. But I have to decide soon. Another layer of pressure. I wanted to come here this summer to gain some perspective. I'm flat burned out with everything. I know my parents love me and want the best for me. But it's as if they push, push, push all the time."

"It sounds like what they want is for you to follow the path they've laid down. Adult children can't always do that and be true to themselves and what they want. My granddad wanted my father to be a farmer. He tried, hated it and went to work in the mines which he liked, odd as it seems. He'd probably be alive today if he'd become a farmer. Then Granddad wanted me to be a farmer, but that's not the life I want. I don't mind helping him out from time to time, but that's not something I'm going to do. Hard for him to accept, but he has. If I ever get married and have children, I will not expect them to go into construction or become a sculptor. Each person has to choose his or her own paths in life. Your decision this summer is, which path are you going to choose?"

For a moment he thought she might say she would choose to remain in Smoky Hollow. She looked out the window at the town and a small smile tugged at her lips. Small and rural, Smoky Hollow had all he wanted. But how could it compete with New York City, or London or Paris?

"I'll have to decide, won't I? No more coasting along."

He wished he could magically find something to say that would have her embracing Smoky Hollow. Have her at least think about staying. Think about him.

Angelica was a long time falling asleep that night. She wandered in the music room and played a few songs, but was too restless to continue. Looking out the window, she saw the light on in Kirk's studio and wished she dared go over and watch him work. But her heart couldn't bear another directive like the other night to go home.

The problem was she wasn't sure exactly where home was. Was it her apartment in New York? The old brownstone home she'd grown up in in Boston? Or was it someplace she hadn't found yet, where she would feel a connection, a rightness that settled all questions.

She liked Smoky Hollow, but how could she make a living here? She was a concert violinist, not a teacher. She'd trained for years, but the thought of more concerts, more practice, more of the same made her tired.

Yet the idea of achieving a tour of Europe in the fall brought a heady rush. It'd be quite an achievement at her age. Hadn't she been working toward something like that her entire life? Could she turn her back on that?

Kirk was right. She stood on a precipice, her entire future ahead of her. But for a moment, she did not want to return to the forest of the familiar. She wanted to be brave enough to step out in a new direction and risk falling flat on her face.

Where was her place?

The next morning Angelica awoke with a vague feeling of dread. Realizing it was apprehension at time running out on her decision for the future, she slowly rose and tried to think of ways to make the right choice. There were so many variables.

First her parents. She'd done her best to please them all her life. Kirk was right, it was time she made her own decisions. Yet she didn't want to hurt them.

Then her agent. He'd taken her on right out of the conservatory, green and new. Worked with her to build a career that others envied. One from which she fled this summer as the pressure built.

She was still dithering about her choice when the phone rang shortly before ten. She hesitated long and hard before answering. She was not ready to give her decision.

"Angelica."

Her father was calling.

"Hi, Dad." Had her mother prevailed upon him to call?

"Your mother told me of your conversation. Honey, we want what's best for you. But it's time you decide that for yourself. Only you will know what's best for you."

She was dumbfounded. They were leaving the decision to her? Just like that? No pressure? No arguments on what they knew was best for her? She didn't know what to say.

"Tell me about the place you're staying this summer," he invited.

Slowly she began to tell him about meeting the warm and friendly residents of this small town. Of the two children she was fast coming to adore. Of Hiram Devon and his amazing voice.

Of Kirk she said little. She dare not chance revealing how much she was coming to rely on him to be there for her.

"Sounds like you are having the time of your life," her father said some time later.

"I guess I am," she said slowly, realization dawning.

She was having a wonderful summer. Glancing out the window she smiled at the trees that shaded the back yard.

"You'll make the right decision. Let us know."

She felt like a prisoner released from jail. What had prompted the call? She didn't want to question her good fortune at not having to convince them she needed to stay, but she didn't understand this abrupt about face at all.

"It was good to talk to you, Dad," she said.

"I enjoyed hearing everything. Do well at your music festival."

She hung up. What had happened? Did her mother know her father had called her? She sat down at the kitchen table and considered the odd conversation. Her mother had been the driving force behind her rise to prominence in the music world, she realized. Her father had always supported her, but never pushed as hard as her mother. Had her father learned something in her determination, in the change in her, from her talk with her mother? It was as if he was giving Angelica permission to be free.

When the phone rang again, she was sure it was her mother, about to give her a different directive. Or her agent, demanding an answer.

"Hello?"

"Hi, Angelica, it's Gina. There's a practice called for this afternoon in the school multi-use room at two. Can you join us? It'll give you a chance to see the various groups who'll be in the festival and meet everyone. Sorry for the late notice, but the gal arranging it all didn't have you on her list."

"Yes, at two. Where is the school?"

Gina rattled off directions and then said how pleased she was that Angelica would be there.

Angelica wondered if Sam knew about the rehearsal. It would be too heartbreaking for him to be practicing so long and not be included. But he was going to the fair today. Still, she wanted him to know about the rehearsal. She knew his last name was Tanner, but looking in the thin phone book that served for Bryceville, Smoky Hollow and three other communities, she saw a dozen Tanners.

She'd have to ask Kirk.

Walking over to his house, Angelica went to the back door and knocked. After a few minutes, she wondered if he could hear someone knocking. She opened the door and peeped in. The kitchen was immaculate. She heard no sounds in the house.

She turned and walked to the studio. The door was closed. When she opened it, the studio was in darkness. No Kirk.

So much for finding out who Sam's father was.

As she started walking back to her house, she heard his motorcycle. She changed directions and went to the back door. A moment later Kirk pulled up. He took off his helmet and looked at her.

"Need something?"

"Sam Tanner's phone number. There's a rehearsal today and I don't want him to miss it."

"Sure, Sam's a third, I think. Anyway, his dad is Sam, too. I've got his number, come on in."

He got off the motorcycle and hung the helmet from the handlebars.

"You were out early," she commented.

"I had breakfast with Granddad," he said as he held the back door open for her.

"How is he?"

"Doing well. And talking about that song you two are doing. He said to ask you to come out tomorrow or the next day if you can."

He pulled open a drawer and rummaged around the papers, pulling out a list of names and numbers.

"Here, Sam senior's the fourth one down."

"What's this list?" she asked, taking the page and scanning all the names.

"Different skills guys have in construction so I know who to call when we have a barn raising like we did for Ben and Carrie. Or some other project. Sam's specialty is electrical. You can use my phone."

He pointed to the phone on the wall.

Once she'd spoken to Sam's mother and told her about the rehearsal she hung up and turned to Kirk.

"My dad called this morning. He practically told me to disregard anything they've said in the past and go for what I want. I couldn't believe it."

He leaned against the kitchen counter and crossed his arms over his chest, tilting his head a little to study her.

"Why? He's an adult, and seems to realize you are one as well."

"He asked about my visit."

"And?"

"So I told him and he said I sounded happy. He's right. I'm happy here."

"You sound almost surprised."

"I guess I am."

"Need a ride to the rehearsal?" he asked.

She considered the offer. One time he tells her to go home, then he takes her to dinner. Now he's offering to take her to the rehearsal. She was confused by the way he acted.

She wasn't confused about wanting to spend as much time with him as she could.

"I'd like that."

"When is it?"

"At two at the high school."

"I'll pick you up about ten minutes before that. It's a short drive."

"It's a short drive anywhere in Smoky Hollow. I could probably walk."

"No need to carry your fiddle all that way."

She should leave. She had nothing else to say, but didn't want to walk away. Finally as the silence stretched out, she smiled and turned to leave.

Kirk watched her go. Once the screen door banged shut behind her he let out his breath. Ever since Angelica Cannon had shown up in Smoky Hollow, his life had been topsy-turvy and didn't seem about to settle down.

Once the festival was over, she' go back where she belonged.

Every time he repeated it, he tried to convince himself that maybe she'd stay. Yet what did he have to offer? His own mother hadn't stayed. Neither he nor his father had meant enough to her.

Much as he wished Angelica would stay, it'd be a waste of her talent, and the prospects for the future. He wasn't going to stand in her way.

Deliberately refusing to look out the window to watch her walk across the lawn, he turned instead to head to the studio. He had several hours before he saw her again. Time enough to shore up defenses.

There were more people than Angelica expected when she reached the school yard where the rehearsal would be held. Her violin was in her case. She brought the one Sam was using in another case, and sheet music for both of them in her tote.

Gina spotted her as soon as Kirk's truck pulled in and hurried over.

"You staying?" she asked Kirk.

"No. How long?"

"Two-three hours. We'll call you."

With that her attention shifted to Angelica.

"Glad you could make it. Come and meet the others."

By the time a modicum of order was established, Angelica had met at least two dozen people. Some names she knew, some she'd never remember. Gina had all the groups lined up together, pointing to spots on the ground where she'd put papers with giant numbers. For the single players, she had them gather in one group. Just as Angelica looked for Sam, a pickup arrived and the little boy jumped out and ran to her.

He looked around.

"There're a lot of people."

His eyes were wide as he took in the crowd.

"And every one will be pleased to hear you play," she assured him, handing him his fiddle. "Just pay attention to the music and the fiddle and pretend it's just you and me."

He looked dubious but nodded.

"Kay," he said.

Gina called for quiet and then read out the roster.

"Everyone just sit where you are until time to do your bit," she concluded.

Angelica sat on the grass, bemused to think of how they rehearsed for the philharmonic. She almost laughed thinking of how the others would be astonished to just sit on the grass until it was time to perform.

One by one the groups played. She loved the jugs and washboard band. The bluegrass group with banjos, drums and fiddles had her keeping time to the lively music. As the afternoon rolled on, she noticed how everyone joined in the spirit of things, clapping along, laughing, cheering.

At last it was the turn of the individuals.

"This is not the order we'll do for the actual performance," Gina said, coming to stand near their group. "I plan to intersperse individuals between the groups. But for today I just want a feeling of how everything sounds. Bob, you and your harmonica are first up."

The haunting melody of "Shenandoah" soon filled the field. At the conclusion everyone cheered.

"Okay, Sam Tanner—you're on," Gina said with a smile.

He rose, took the fiddle from the case and the music. Shyly looking around, he looked at Angelica for support.

She smiled encouragingly.

"You can do it, Sam. Make me proud."

The little boy set his music, placed the fiddle beneath his chin and began the song he'd practiced all summer. Soon people were clapping, smiling, calling encouragement. He finished to a huge ovation and beamed his pride at Angelica.

"I knew you could to it, Sam. You'll be a smash at the festival."

She gave him a quick hug.

"You're up next, Angelica."

Suddenly a wave a stage fright threatened to choke her. She stood, feeling as awkward and nervous as at her audition for the philharmonic.

"You can do it, Miss Cannon," Sam whispered.

She smiled at him. He was right, she could.

"I thought I'd do two, if that's okay," she said to Gina.

At her nod, Angelica began one of her solo pieces from the last symphony. The haunting music filled the area and she glanced around, trying to gauge the reaction of the rest of the performers. Most were smiling. Odd how she could see everyone. When the song ended, applause was heartfelt.

Putting the violin in place a second time, she began Orange Blossom Special.

It was fast and furious and she'd have liked more practice but as she played the rest of the performers began clapping, whistling and calling encouragement. She relaxed and began to enjoy herself. Letting her gaze sweep the crowd she realized she was part of a gathering of people who shared the same love of music and made that love known. Halfway through someone yelled out, "Faster!"

She looked around, not sure who it was, but she'd give it her best. Increasing the tempo she met a roar of approval from everyone. Faster and faster she played the now familiar song until she reached the end.

The applause was amazing. She grinned and held her violin up like a trophy. Those sitting stood, the clapping went on and on and the calls for do it again began to swell.

Gina came to give her a hug.

"Always a crowd pleaser. Can you do it again?"

"Sure."

It was more fun than anything she'd ever done with the violin. She played the song again and the crowd showed its delight. She'd never felt the give and take in a performance like she did today. It was heady beyond belief.

She sat down after that, even though several people asked for something else.

"Okay, let's not overwhelm our guest," Gina said with a broad smile. "She'll play at the festival. Mary Margaret, you're up next."

"Don't know if I want to follow her," the librarian said with a smile for Angelica.

She had a guitar and soon began to sing a sad ballad of lost love.

Sam scooted over close to Angelica.

"Thank you for helping me," he whispered.

She reached out and gave him a hug.

It's my pleasure and delight."

After everyone had played, Gina declared the rehearsal a success and scheduled one for the day before the event, when they'd play in order of the festival.

Rachel Tanner appeared for Sam. When she heard Angelica would have to call Kirk for a ride, she insisted on taking her home.

"Mom, I did good. And everyone clapped," Sam said, jumping excitedly.

"He did amazing. We all loved it," Angelica said when she was in the truck, the little boy between her and his mom, both violin cases in her lap.

"Webb Francis said he has some aptitude for it. Thank you for letting him practice even with Webb Francis gone," Rachel Tanner said. "We sure do appreciate it."

"He'll go far if he wants," Angelica said.

Was this how her professors felt when she achieved some honor? When they knew they'd been instrumental in helping her along such a demanding career?

She was as happy for Sam as she was for her own performance.

"Miss Cannon played Orange Blossom Special and then she played it really fast."

"I love that song. That's your piece for the festival?" Rachel asked.

"Yes, one of them. And one from a classical selection."

"You'll be a big hit with that one. I'll love to hear one of the songs you play in New York," she said.

Angelica was pleased with the way the day had gone. Very different from the rehearsals for the orchestra.

Once dropped off at the house, she went in and put the violins away, then looked over at Kirk's house. She was too excited not to share. A minute later she was peeping into the open door of the studio. He was working on the sculpture and she paused a moment to watch him before he knew she was there.

She felt a yearning for things that couldn't be. How wonderful to rush to share her day with him. To learn what he'd done. To watch as he made beauty from chunks of wood. To have him sweep her up in a hug and kiss.

She could only see a partial side view of his face, but the concentration was evident. He put down the chisel and took some sandpaper, rubbing it gently along the line he'd just carved. His hands were steady and skilled. She could watch him for hours. But the bubbling excitement from the day couldn't be contained.

"Kirk," she said, stepping inside.

He looked up.

"Back already? How did it go? How did you get home?"

"Sam's mother gave me a lift. It was wonderful. I loved hearing all the music, watching everyone playing. It was amazing."

She came to the table and looked at the art work. She could see the woman in the lone figure, see the trees both welcoming and a bit foreboding. How did he manage that?

"This is wonderful. I can really see the shape now," she said reaching out to touch lightly.

His work called for touch.

"It's coming along. Tell me about the practice."

She beamed at him.

"Totally unlike any rehearsal I've been to. It was such fun. The songs were different from what I'm used to it was like magic. I couldn't have imagined it before. Now I wonder if I can go back to the philharmonic. In comparison, it doesn't come close. We sat on the grass and everyone encouraged everyone else. It was wild and a bit uncontrolled, but loads of fun."

"Music is music, different tastes for different folks," he said. "Think of all the pleasure you give to those who attend the symphony."

"I guess. But it's hard slogging through hours of practice every day. It's more of a job than a love. Today was about loving to share music."

"You've been practicing since you've been here. What's different from back in New York?"

"It's just different."

She picked up a chisel and looked at it, placing it gently back on the table.

"Here it's pure fun. Trying new songs, mastering intricate melodies. I played Orange Blossom Special and everyone was smiling and laughing, clapping. Urging me on. I felt like everyone there was sending vibes to encourage me. That is not something I get at practice in New York."

He shrugged, watching her with that intensity she now expected.

"Sam was wonderful," she continued. "He started out a bit shy and nervous, but soon was fully into the song and everyone was as encouraging for him as for everyone else. It didn't matter he's only eight or this was his first try."

She swept her arms wide.

"This was the best day!"

Her hands dropped to her sides.

"And you made it possible," she said smiling broadly at him.

"I didn't do anything," he said.

"You believed in me and my right to make my own decisions. That's special. You're coming to the festival, right?"

He hesitated for a moment and Angelica remembered his hearing loss. Maybe it wasn't as much fun if the music couldn't be heard in full range. But she really wanted him to hear her play. If he sat near the front, she'd play right to him.

"Sure, I'll be there."

Kirk watched as she continued to talk about her amazing day. His heart ached with desire to pull her into his arms, to kiss her in celebration. Hear every detail. She was so happy. He wanted to always remember her just like this. Completely content and happy in the day.

In the months and years ahead, he'd always pull out this memory when thinking of Angelica. Years wouldn't dim the happiness. Time wouldn't tarnish this perfect moment. He imprinted it forever on his mind.

She stopped talking and cocked her head to the left.

"Are you listening to me?"

He nodded, wishing she'd stay forever, knowing she couldn't. Her future did not lie in Smoky Hollow.

Chapter Ten

When Angelica left a short time later, Kirk leaned against the table, feeling as if he'd run a marathon. The effort to keep from touching her had been tremendous. But he couldn't get more involved. He remembered how he'd felt when Alice returned his ring. The message had been clear—there was more she wanted from life than him.

If he'd gone after her, would that have changed any thing?

But he hadn't.

He hadn't known Angelica nearly as long as he'd known Alice. This burning in his blood for her could be extinguished in a short order. It only felt deeper and stronger than what he'd felt for Alice because it was fresh and immediate.

Once she left—he didn't want to think about that day. Get through this one. Focus on his work. Ignore the clamoring of his senses to spend more time with her. Dinner together would be nice. Maybe some dancing so he could hold her close, breathe in the sweet scent of her, memorize the feel of her body against his. He knew she wasn't very worldly in her personal life. Could he be the one to show her how passion could spark and flare between them?

He didn't need dancing, he felt as if every inch of her had been imprinted on him when they'd kissed.

He picked up the sandpaper, not trusting himself just yet with a sharp tool that could gouge as wrongly as certainly as it could the way he wanted. Slowly he let the rhythm of sanding soothe his blood. He could do this. She'd be gone soon.

The days might be tough to get through initially, but before Christmas, she'd only be a vague memory. Okay, maybe by next summer.

He threw down the paper in disgust. He was never ever going to forget Angelica Cannon. Closing the studio, he headed out. Maybe his granddad would welcome some company for supper.

When he called him, Hiram answered right away.

"Sure, come on over. Bring that New York gal with you. I've found some more music for her. Songs my mother sang when I was a boy. Seeing them again reminded me of her voice, like an angel."

Kirk almost groaned in defeat. Even his grandfather was working against him. He couldn't very well explain why he didn't want to be around Angelica. That'd give rise to speculation he could do without. No sympathy this time around when nursing a broken heart. He'd had more than enough of that with Alice's defection.

"I'll ask her, she may have other plans."

"What could she be doing in Smoky Hollow that you wouldn't already know?" his grandfather asked.

"I don't keep track of her every moment," Kirk responded—though he'd like to.

"I heard the festival participants had a rehearsal today," Hiram said.

Kirk never ceased to be amazed at how much his grandfather knew without ever stepping foot in town.

"She loved it," he said.

"Figured she would. She can tell me over dinner. I'll put on the barbecue, you can cook."

Kirk gave in with as much grace as he could muster. "Okay. We'll be over around six."

Angelica had been delighted to accept the invitation when Kirk called her. He rolled out his motorcycle and went to pick her up shortly before six.

She was still excited about her afternoon.

"I can tell your grandfather all about it. I still want him to sing at the festival. Do you think he will?" she asked as she put on the helmet.

"No, but you can ask."

As if they'd been riding partners for years, she easily slid into the space behind him and wrapped her arms around him. He could have taken the truck. She never would have been this close in the truck.

Her arms were warm, her hands clenched across his belly. He wanted to impress the feeling of her breasts pressing against his back. Turn and pull her into his arms and kiss her until they both forgot the day.

Instead he tried to concentrate on driving and ignore the heated blood that shot through his veins.

Hiram was watching for them and came out as soon as they drove into the yard. His dog barked a welcome and danced around them, stirring dust in the air.

"Hey, missy, tell me how things went at the rehearsal," he greeted her as soon as Kirk stopped.

For the next few minutes Kirk sat on the bike, watching as Angelica charmed his grandfather with her enthusiasm and honest assessment of everything she'd seen. She was high on praise and brought in slyly that another singer was needed in her opinion to balance things out.

"I could put in a good word for you with Gina," she ended, grinning at Hiram.

Kirk watched as his grandfather seemed to consider the suggestion. Could he really think about singing in the festival again?

The three of them prepared dinner. Angelica insisting on helping. When they sat around the old farm table, Kirk tried to remember the last time a woman had been there for dinner.

Hiram was as animated as Kirk had ever seen. Her visit was good for the old man. He hoped she'd remember them once in a while in the years ahead and maybe drop a note.

"So you see, you're needed," she concluded when she finished another plea for his singing. "I think you should sing that song you told me the words to. Could I learn the music in time do you think? I hunted around and actually found the sheet music in Webb Francis's stack. I could accompany you."

Hiram looked at Kirk.

"What do you think?"

"About her learning the music, from what I know she can practically hear a song once and play it. Do you want to sing?"

Hiram looked back and forth between them.

"Maybe I do."

"Wonderful. Let's call Gina right now. Do you have her number?" she asked, looking at Kirk.

"It's in the book. Really, Granddad?"

"Don't you think I can?" he asked testily.

"I think it would be a miracle and a wonderful one at that," Kirk said.

"Call her. See what she says," Hiram instructed Angelica.

Ten minutes later a smiling Angelica hung up the phone.

"She's thrilled. Says that'll get even more people there."

"Coming to see if I still have the voice, I expect," Hiram said wryly.

She laughed.

"You'll show them. Shall I practice to accompany you?"

"Sure, who else would I want?"

"Let's see what we have, so I can start in the morning," she said.

"I'll clean up," Kirk offered as they both rose to go to the front of the house to discuss the music.

He did the dishes, walked outside to check on things around the farm. The fence had been reinforced. The hogs seemed happy enough in their large pens. He rested a foot on a lower bar and leaned against it, looking at the darkening sky.

He mentally counted the days until the festival. Could he last that long? Maybe he'd take a quick trip to Atlanta and visit the gallery there that carried his work. See what the feedback was from patrons and get some ideas for another sculpture.

Or he could stay at home, work on the woman on the precipice carving and deal with having Angelica close for another couple of weeks and practice saying goodbye so when the time came, he wouldn't blow it.

The next morning Kirk had hardly finished his coffee when the phone rang. It was his grandfather.

"I'm coming in to see Angelica, we're going to practice in Webb Francis's music room. She has students coming this afternoon, so we're going to claim mornings for our practice."

"Good."

"Let's have lunch. She said you have an amazing sculpture

you're working on. Can an old man see it?"

"Anytime, you know that. If I'm in the studio, come on in. I might need to be interrupted to remember it's lunchtime."

His grandfather would spend hours with Angelica over the next weeks. If he could hear, if he could sing, he could have been the one volunteering for the festival, just to spend time with her. He envied his grandfather.

How pathetic was that.

The next week passed quickly. Kirk grew used to his grandfather coming to visit Angelica every morning. In the afternoon she had Teresa Ann and Sam over to practice. Kirk rarely saw her. Which, he tried to convince himself, was exactly what he wanted.

He took on another job helping a renovation with a family on the far side of town. It was exasperating work, with the other workers constantly trying his patience. Evenings he worked on his sculpture. In between, he stayed as far from home as he could.

Not seeing her every day didn't diminish the yearning to be with her, however. Much as he hoped out of sight, out of mind would be the norm, it didn't work that way.

Ten days after his grandfather began practicing with Angelica, Kirk rode over to the farm early to share breakfast with him.

"You've been busy," Hiram said when they sat down to eat.

Kirk nodded.

"Angelica said she hadn't seen you. She's busy, too, of course, getting ready for the festival," Hiram continued.

Kirk watched him a moment.

"Are you still singing?"

Hiram nodded.

"We've got it all squared away. You coming?"

Kirk nodded.

"Said I would. I'd like to hear you sing again. Those are good memories I had from when I was a kid."

When he never thought of the future, never considered life wouldn't go along as good as he'd had back then. For a moment he wished he could turn back the clock.

Yet, would he really do anything differently? He'd still serve his country in the military, still be partially deaf. Maybe he'd have let Angelica get off the bus and find her way.

No, that would never have happened. No use wishing for the past. It wouldn't change a thing.

"Hope you can hear me well enough," the old man said.

They rarely talked about Kirk's lack of hearing, but his comment warmed Kirk. He hoped he could hear both Hiram and Angelica—enough to appreciate their skills. He knew he'd hear the applause when they finished.

"Jody Miller called a couple of days ago, asking me if you were off your feed or something."

"Why would he call you? I've been working on a renovation project at his place."

"I know, and he said you're acting like a bear with a sore paw. Something eating at you?"

Kirk shrugged.

"A pretty gal from New York, maybe?" his grandfather guessed.

"She'll be gone soon."

"And that's what's eating at you, right?"

Kirk looked at the older man, then sighed and nodded.

"She's a looker and has a sweet disposition. Reminds me a bit of your grandma when she was young and sassy. I did that all wrong. Regretted it all these years," Hiram said slowly.

Kirk was staggered. His grandfather never spoke of his wife.

Kirk had never heard him say he regretted things—or that he might be at fault.

"Devon men just can't keep their women," Kirk said.

"If I'd treated her better, she might have stayed. Not so with your mother, I don't think. Your dad did all he could for her— she flat-out didn't want to stay in Smoky Hollow."

"Like Alice."

"Yes, but that gal was restless from the get-go. Think back, all through high school she talked of going someplace else."

"So did I. And I went. Found I like this place best."

"Alice needed that chance. Only when she took it, she didn't like Smoky Hollow best. You don't have to stay here, Kirk. You're young, you can do your wood sculptures anywhere, work construction anywhere like you did before. If there's something sizzling between you and Angelica, don't let it go."

"I've never heard you talk like this," Kirk said.

"A man gets to being old and alone and thinks back to how he might have changed things in the past."

"I don't see as how I'd change anything," Kirk said.

"I do. A whole lot. And maybe your dad would be alive today, and maybe I'd have had a house full of young'uns. Can't change it now, of course. But don't you make my mistakes. Go after what you want. And make sure anything holding you back is real and not pride or false values. You hear me?"

Kirk nodded.

"We'll see," he said.

He didn't like the way the conversation was going so he changed the topic to farm matters. Easier to deal with his grandfather on routine matters. Just before he was set to leave, Hiram looked at him.

"Have you heard from Webb Francis?"

"Yeah, the other day. He's doing better. Plans to be at the festival. Front row seat, he says."

"Is he going to play?"

"Not this year, but he's anticipating hearing Angelica. He wondered if she'd do a classical piece as well. That's what she plays in New York."

"I asked her. She is," Hiram said.

"Be something to hear, I expect."

He just hoped he could.

Kirk went to the library after leaving the farm, to use the Internet. He searched on Angelica's name and was surprised to find how many references he found. Reading through the first dozen or so, he realized how valuable a member she was of the philharmonic—a true rising star. The accolades were heartfelt. The fame of his young neighbor apparently was well established in the music community of New York and parts of Europe.

The last bit of wishful hope that she'd consider staying in Smoky Hollow died.

And he'd be doing her and the music world a disservice to even ask her to stay. She had a bright future. This visit was a short stretch out of time.

He should make the most of it instead of ignoring what was right in front of him. There were two weeks left before the festival. Once that was past, she'd be gone. Could he deal with fourteen days of Angelica and then let her go?

Could he regret not spending those days with her for the rest of his life?

Angelica heard the knock on the door as she was finishing making her sandwich. She went to the front door. Kirk stood there.

"Busy?" he asked.

She hadn't seen him for a week and now he shows up as if yesterday was the last time he'd seen her.

"I'm fixing lunch."

He stayed silent, looking at her intensely like he did. Her attraction for him had not diminished one iota during the absence. Her body seemed to sing now that he was here. His wide shoulders had her longing to reach out and drag him in. His slow smile had her insides doing flip-flops.

"Want to eat with me?" she said finally when he hadn't broken the silence.

"Sure."

He opened the screen door and stepped into the room. He seemed to crowd her even with a couple of feet of space between them.

Angelica spun around and hurried to the kitchen, glad for the task of making another sandwich to give her something to do.

"I'm surprised to see you," she said as she placed the sandwiches on plates and put them on the table.

He sat and watched her.

"I've been working on a renovation the other side of town. And working on the carving."

"How is that now?"

"Coming along. Want to come over and see it after lunch?"

"I could," she said cautiously.

Once they began eating, she couldn't let her curiosity stay quiet.

"Why are you here?"

"To see you."

"I thought you told me to go home."

He shrugged.

"You will after the festival. Until then, why not spend time together?"

She could think of a dozen reasons, the primary one being how she was falling in love with the man. She'd learned a lot these few weeks. She liked the people she met. She liked dealing with children. There were different ways to live from the way she lived.

Whether she'd want a permanent change was still up in the air. She didn't dislike every part of her life in New York. Would she completely be accepted in Smoky Hollow, or was she here on sufferance because of Webb Francis and Kirk?

And in the greater scheme, hadn't she come here to find out what a different way of life was like? How could she know if she didn't take every opportunity offered?

Who knew? Maybe a miracle would happen and he'd fall in love with her and they'd share their lives together.

"Doing what?" she asked.

"I thought we could go into Bryceville later, have dinner at a great barbecue place I know and then see if there's a movie in town we'd want to see."

There was no skating around that. It was a date.

She nodded.

"So tell me, how are the kids doing with their lessons?" he asked.

They talked about Sam and Teresa Ann, moving on to the topic of Hiram's big comeback, as Angelica called it.

"He blows me away with his voice. Age has not diminished it at all. He'll wow the crowd."

"Webb Francis seems to think you will."

She shrugged.

"I've been practicing."

"Pops said you're doing a solo from one of your concerts," he said slowly.

"And?"

She seemed defensive.

"I think we'll be fortunate to hear you."

She thought it over.

"Sam's mom said the same thing."

They'd enjoy anything she played, he thought. He would, even if he couldn't hear it all. Watching her would be enough.

Angelica dressed with care for her date. She didn't have much variety, but so far neither had anyone else in town shown a huge wardrobe. The pink of her cotton top enhanced the color she'd picked up from the sun, making her blue eyes look brighter. Or was it the anticipation in seeing Kirk again?

She waited on the front porch and heard the muffled roar of the motorcycle when he started it. Smiling she waited. The things she did here would have astonished her six months ago, six weeks ago. Now she agreed with what Kirk and Webb Francis had said that first morning—the back of a motorcycle was the best way to see things.

The ride into Bryceville was fun. She held on, savoring every movement of his body as he smoothly leaned into curves. They couldn't talk, but she didn't need conversation. Being with him was enough.

She was so glad he'd stopped by at lunch. Her time was winding down and decisions had to be made soon. But for today, she'd go with the flow and savor every second.

The barbecue was delicious and messy. They used a dozen napkins and she still had to stop and wash her hands before they headed for the movie theater. The feature movie was a comedy. As they waited in line to buy their tickets, a very short line compared to the lines she'd seen in New York, she asked if he could hear film soundtracks.

"Most of it. The theater cranks up the sound pretty loud. Sometimes I miss parts. I don't come often," he said.

He touched her back as they moved forward, sending spiraling shivers down her spine. They found seats near the center. The theater wasn't crowded, though the air-conditioning felt so good Angelica thought everyone around should come for the relief from the heat.

Kirk held the popcorn in his lap, near her so she could easily reach for some. The lights dimmed and the coming attractions began. Halfway through the box of popcorn, she reached in and tangled her fingers with his. Startled, she looked at him. He looked back and smiled, withdrawing his hand.

Disappointed, she took another few kernels and then whispered, "I'm finished. I can't believe I ate anything after dinner."

He set the box on the floor by his feet and reached for her hand as casually and confidently as if they'd held hands forever.

Angelica drew in a sharp breath, feeling every cell in her body focus on Kirk. She couldn't get back into the story unfolding on the screen. She could only feel the hardness of his palm, the callouses on his fingers as they gently cradled hers. He rested their linked hands on his thigh. A surreptitious glance showed he was watching the movie. Didn't he feel the charge?

Gradually her heart rate settled down and she picked up the threads of the movie, but she never grew complacent about their linked hands.

It was dark on the ride home. The air was cooler, scented with night smells. What mysteries lurked in the darkened woods that lined the road? Who else was out, enjoying the brilliance of the stars, the lessening of the day's heat? She felt magical gliding through the night with skin brushed by the air, her head dancing with fantasies.

When they reached the cottage, she climbed off the

motorcycle reluctantly. She could have ridden to California and back and still not had enough.

"That was fun," she said, walking to the door.

"You didn't leave a light on," he said.

"I didn't think about it when it was still light. I know right where the switch is," she replied, unwilling to end the evening. "Want to come in for coffee?"

"Another time. I have another work day tomorrow on the Millers' place."

He drew her slowly into his arms and kissed her. Angelica closed her eyes and let the magic of the moment sweep her away. Kirk made her feel like the most precious thing on earth.

Angelica didn't know what changed Kirk's mind, but the next few days were more fun than she'd ever had in her life. They went back to the waterfall and pool. She still didn't have a bathing suit, but it didn't matter. They enjoyed another picnic and splashed each other until they were sopping wet.

They walked to the general store one afternoon and got ice cream cones, trying to lick the ice cream before it could melt in the heat and run down their arms.

Kirk took her on several hikes through the forests. She relished the bird songs, the soft rustle of the leaves and the dappled shade. Appreciating them even more knowing he didn't hear them. She couldn't imagine not hearing. How would she live without music or the other sounds that were in her life?

Another thunderstorm had them cooking on an open fire, kissing, talking about anything that came up, and kissing. She was beginning to wish there'd be more storms—as long as she lived next door to Kirk. He never pushed her, never took her for granted. She fell more and more in love which made the decisions that much harder.

Time was running out. Her agent was pressuring her to get back to New York and begin rehearsals. She'd never formally accepted the tour, holding off just in case there was another major change in her life—like Kirk falling in love with her.

But much as she enjoyed being with him, she saw nothing in him that gave her hope.

Still, she spent as much time as she could when he asked her out. They had to work around practice with the children and with Hiram. Plus her own practice. But they had plenty of quiet time together.

She loved to wander to the studio and watch him work. The sculpture was amazing. The individual trees now showed definite detail. The figure on the brink was still untouched. He said he was keeping that fine detail work until last. He wouldn't be finished before she left.

Would he send her a picture when it was complete? She asked, he said yes, but the answer was vague and didn't satisfy her. Maybe she'd get his grandfather to promise.

Every day he held hands, kissed her, and sometimes she didn't think he'd let her go. She was so deep in love by the day before the music festival she couldn't think straight. She wanted Kirk to be proud of her at the festival. But how much could he really hear? Would he enjoy it as much as she hoped all the others would?

She was also nervous for Sam. The hours he'd put into practice really paid off. He was as ready as could be, but the last couple of days he'd seemed reluctant. He wasn't getting stage fright, was he?

At least she didn't have to worry about Hiram getting stage fright. He talked about showing off to Marlene Parker every day. If nothing else, he'd do it to prove to that woman that the feud from years gone by was over. And he came out on top. Angelica wondered what caused the feud, but he never told her, just kept saying wait until Marlene saw him singing again.

The afternoon before the festival it rained. Sam came dragging in trailing his umbrella. He was soaked.

"You need to dry off before you can use the fiddle," she said, surprised at how wet he was.

"I might get a cold and be sick tomorrow," he said, eyeing the violin with some trepidation.

"Even with a cold, you can play. Unless you break all your fingers and your jaw, you can play," she said leaning over to look him right in the eye. "It's what we do as musicians. We play when we said we would. People are coming from all over to hear you. How would you feel if you went someplace expecting something and it wasn't there?"

"Everybody plays better."

"Not true. Most people in the audience couldn't play a single note. They love to listen to music, but they can't make it. There are some there better than you, some worse. Some have studied longer, but you have talent and the desire to succeed."

She brushed his damp hair off his forehead.

"You know I'm leaving in a couple of days," she said.

"I don't want you to go," he said looking so woebegone she almost smiled.

She wished Kirk had said those words.

"I know, but my life is back in New York. I've had a wonderful vacation here. And I'll always remember our practicing together. So you have to do one more thing for me and play your very best tomorrow."

He nodded, scuffing his wet sneakers.

"I wish you'd stay here. What if Webb Francis doesn't want to teach me? What if he won't teach Teresa Ann?"

She hugged the child, wondering the same thing.

"He will."

She hoped she was right.

"Ick, you're all wet," she said, stepping back.

He giggled.

"Come on back and you can have some milk and cookies and I'll dry your shirt in the dryer."

It was bittersweet watching him practice for the last time. She'd never thought she'd enjoy teaching so much. She was as proud of him as she would have been of her own mastering of a difficult piece.

Teresa Ann showed up and the two children squabbled and practiced and both asked her to stay and never go away.

Angelica hugged them both when they left, promising to meet them at the festival. She and Teresa Ann were going to be backstage when Sam played.

Kirk came over after the children left. She was going to miss him even more than the children. She didn't want to think about that. Despite her earlier assertion, she'd fallen big time for this man.

And he'd never even hinted she should stay.

"Want to go for a ride?" he asked.

"Sure."

The last few days were hard to live through. She was saving up memories like mad. She didn't want to forget a single moment of her wonderful summer.

A short time later they were flying along the quiet country road, wind seeping beneath the helmet, warm and humid. Clouds built in the west. Another storm? Or would it blow north of them? The green trees sped by, and the air was fragrant, rich and moist.

Angelica hugged Kirk, relishing the feel of him against her, wishing they could ride like this forever.

She'd never forget her summer in Smoky Hollow.

Would she come back?

It might be too hard to see Kirk again once she was used to not being with him. Better for her state of mind to focus on where to go next and not yearn for the impossible.

She had the tour in Europe, another season with the symphony. Other concerts.

Somehow the future didn't look as exciting as it once had.

It was dusk when they returned. Rumblings in the distance signaled the storm was heading their way. Would they lose power like the last time?

He drove up to his house and stopped.

"Come in and eat with me," he invited. "Or we could go to the diner."

"Don't you think it's going to rain soon? Probably safer to stay here."

They prepared the meal together, she making the salad and setting the table, Kirk grilling two steaks and corn on the cob. From time to time, Angelica stopped working to look at him. Once he turned his head and caught her gaze.

He cocked an eyebrow in silent question, but she merely shook her head and resumed her task, not wanting him to know she was memorizing every move he made to remember forever.

"Nervous about tomorrow?" he asked when they were eating.

"Not so much. I've done this a lot. Not this song or to this audience. I'm more concerned about Sam. He's practiced so hard. I want him to do well."

"He'll do fine. No one will expect virtuoso level from him. This is his first time and he's only eight."

However they would expect a virtuoso level from her. She sometimes wished she played for fun and not as a career. Could she enjoy it more, be more forgiving of mistakes?

"When are you leaving?" Kirk asked, studying the iced tea in his glass.

She waited until he raised his gaze to hers.

"The day after tomorrow. I have responsibilities that I can't get out of. I wish I could blow them off, but I'm not made that way."

"We knew you'd be leaving," he said, his dark eyes fascinating her.

She wished he'd ask her to stay, or at least say he didn't want her to leave like Sam had.

"Do you ever go to New York?" she asked, desperately longing for something to hold on to.

He hesitated a moment as if in thought, then slowly shook his head.

"This is my place," he said.

She knew that. Here he was needed. Here he could do what he did best, helping his neighbors, making amazing wood sculptures. This was his place.

But it wasn't hers.

"Webb Francis called today, his sister is bringing him early to the festival. He's determined to get a front row seat," she said, deliberately changing the subject before she burst into tears.

"I heard from him, too. We'll probably sit together. I'll be bringing my grandfather. Do you need a ride?"

She shook her head.

"I'm going with Sam and his parents. And Teresa Ann."

When the dishes were done the rain began.

"I'm going to dash home now before it gets worse," she said, watching the first of the drops splash against the kitchen window. The breeze blew it almost sideways.

"You'll get soaked."

"No telling how long it'll last. I can dry off before bed this way."

He walked her to her door, despite her protest he'd get twice as wet. The porch was sheltered from the rain, the sound loud against its roof.

Kirk cradled her head in his hands, his thumbs rubbing lightly against her cheeks as he stared down into her eyes. She could hardly see him in the darkness, only the light from the back of the cottage shone through the windows giving faint illumination.

"You're very special, Angel. I wish for you the best life has to offer."

He kissed her, softly, sweetly. Then dropped his hands.

"See you tomorrow."

She watched as he ran across the lawn and disappeared into the night. His figure was blurred—from the rain or the tears that now fell she wasn't sure.

"I love you," she whispered into the night.

Chapter Eleven

The air was festive, the crowd good-natured and ready for fun. When Angelica and Sam and the Tanner family arrived at the fairgrounds, the parking lot was already half full and the performance wasn't scheduled to start for another hour. They'd arrived early and Angelica was surprised to see so many others had also arrived early. They hurried to the amphitheater and found Gina who was marshaling everyone into places in the lineup.

Sam hugged Webb Francis's violin and stayed so close to Angelica she almost stumbled over him when she turned once.

She looked at him. His eyes were big, watching everything around him, and darting from time to time to the stage. The crowd couldn't be seen from their location, but she could hear the people.

She stooped down and faced him.

"Sam, look at me."

He complied, looking as if he was going to cry.

She smiled gently.

"You are eight years old and performing at your first festival. I want you to remember what a fun time we had all these weeks playing the fiddle. I want you to always remember your first time here. You'll probably play every festival from now until you're as old as Mr. Devon. But this will always be your first time. Have fun, sweetie. Play for me and Teresa Ann and your mom. Don't worry about any one else."

"Maybe Kirk?" he said. "And my dad?"

"Okay, play for them, too. If you start to think of anything else, turn and look at me and only me, got that?"

He nodded solemnly.

"Make me proud," she said, hugging him and then standing. She leaned over and picked her violin case from the grass where she'd dropped it when talking to Sam. Good thing her mother wasn't here to see that. She'd have had a hissy fit.

"Okay everyone, we're about to start. Break a leg," Gina called, shepherding the first group to the edge of the stage.

Sam looked at Angelica.

"Why did she say that?"

"Theater superstition. Do not break anything."

As the afternoon progressed, group after group stepped up, followed each time by a solo act. When it was Sam's turn, Angelica went right to the edge of the stage with him. She could see the crowd now, the amphitheater as full as it had been during the fair. Sam walked on, listened until the introduction was finished and then looked at Angelica. He raised the fiddle and began. He played beautifully.

Tears filled her eyes at the performance. She thought her heart would burst with pride. His gaze never left hers. When he was done, he gave a short bow and scurried off the stage.

"Sweetie, go back, they're clapping for you," she said, turning him around and pushing him back.

His eyes widened in wonder and then he beamed his smile to the audience. The clapping went on for several minutes. He bowed again and then came off stage, grinning from ear to ear.

"I did it!"

"You did great!" She hugged him and then hurried him away as the next group was introduced.

Twenty minutes later Angelica took a breath and stepped out on the stage in Bryceville, Kentucky. There was no darkened theater, but a wide open amphitheater filled to the brim with people who had come to enjoy good music.

She hardly heard the introduction as she sought Kirk and Webb Francis. They were right on the front row, both grinning at her.

She glanced around at the audience. Normally she never saw anyone at the symphonies. Now she could see every person there—even Paul and Melvin. So they did leave the store rocking chairs sometimes.

Glancing to her right, she saw Sam standing by the stage, to give her support, he'd said. If she got scared, she was to look at him. She gave a wink and placed the violin in the familiar spot, rested her bow on it for a second. And began.

Tchaikovsky's solo first movement was one she loved. She played it with as much feeling as she could, to honor all the people who had come so far to hear good music. It was totally different from the others on the program, and she tried to see how well it was going over as she played. But, oddly enough after all these years, she felt nervous.

Seeking Kirk again, she focused on him. The rest of the crowd seem to fade as he smiled slowly. She hoped he heard every note.

When she finished the applause was tremendous. People even stood, clapped and yelled Kirk and Webb Francis among them.

She felt almost giddy with delight that everyone liked the music.

The applause went on for several minutes, finally dying down. She smiled again, nodding to Kirk, and began the song she'd practiced on this summer, Orange Blossom Special. She played it looking directly at Kirk, hoping he could hear her, hoping he liked the song as much as he said he did.

The crowd went wild, clapping and yelling. Obviously a favorite with more than one. Momentarily she glanced around and then grinned, playing for all she was worth. The long notes of the plaintive whistle, then the faster notes as if a train was roaring down the tracks. Clapping went on and faster, so she sped up. The crowd loved it. Finally the song ended, but not the ovation. People called to do it again. Gina nodded from the sidelines, so Angelica played it through a second time, then bowed and left.

"They're still clapping and calling," Sam said. "You should go back out there."

She stepped back in sight and waved her violin and bowed again, then left.

"Excellent," Hiram said, coming up to them.

"I wondered where you were," she said, giving him a quick hug in her exuberance.

"I sat out front, no sense missing all the others by standing around back here."

"You ready?" she asked.

"As I'll ever be. You, Mr. Sam, did a fine job," he said to the boy.

Sam smiled.

"I'm going to play next year, too."

It seemed like only moments later Hiram and Angelica stepped out on the stage. She stood a little behind him and to his right, giving him center stage. He motioned her closer, but she smiled and shook her head, bow poised.

"Ready?" she asked.

He nodded, turned to face the audience.

She bet the old ballad never sounded so good as his strong voice sang of love lost. She watched Kirk as he listened to his grandfather, then he looked at her. For a long moment as the words filled the air, her heart sped up wanting to fly right to his.

Sudden tears filled her eyes as she related to the sad lyrics. She looked away afraid she'd mess up the accompaniment. The crowd was quiet as Hiram sang, but burst into applause and cheers when he finished.

Gina gave him a hug when he came off stage.

"You two are great. Plan on next year," she said.

Angelica was startled. She never thought about coming back.

Hiram nodded, then looked around for Kirk. He came from the audience a moment later.

"You did amazing," he said to his grandfather, giving him a hug.

The old man protested, but the hint of color rising in his face showed his pleasure.

"And you played like an angel," Kirk said to her. "You have an amazing talent. The world will be blessed by your music for many years to come."

She blinked. She hadn't expected that.

"We ready to leave?" Hiram asked.

"Sure." Kirk answered, but his eyes never left hers. "You're still leaving in the morning?"

She nodded.

"Taking the bus."

He hesitated a long moment, glanced around at all the people.

Ask me to stay. Tell me you'll come visit me. Write to me. She wished so hard she wondered if telepathy wouldn't covey her yearning to everyone.

"Have a good trip home," he said.

She nodded and smiled, but her heart ached and tears clogged her throat. But she kept her chin up.

"Thanks for all you've done. Send me a picture of the finished sculpture."

You are the most amazing man, she wanted to say. I wished you loved me.

He nodded.

"Let's go. Them hogs will be hungry," Hiram said.

He looked at Angelica.

"You come back, hear? I might find another song we can do next year."

"I'll keep that in mind," she said, without making any commitment. Tears filled her eyes despite her effort at keeping them at bay.

"Bye, girl," the old man said, pulling her into a hug. "Don't forget us."

She rode home with the Tanners and endured their profuse thanks for helping their son. She bid them goodbye with real regret, hugging Sam extra hard. An entire new world had opened teaching him. Something else to think about in the future.

She took Webb Francis's violin back into the cottage. She had so little to pack, she could do it in the morning. She was taking the bus to Louisville to catch the plane from there. Not much left to do here. The cottage was tidy. She'd change sheets before she left in the morning.

Taking a glass of iced tea to the porch, she sat in the growing twilight thinking about the festival, the friends she'd made in Smoky Hollow. She was even getting used to the humid heat. It was peaceful, serene. So unlike New York City. A place she truly hoped she never forgot. Nor the people. Nor the gentle way of life.

After she was ready for bed she went to the window of her room and stared across the dark to Kirk's house. The light was on in the studio. She wished she could have seen the finished sculpture. She considered going over there now, but it was late and they'd said goodbye earlier, before he took his grandfather home. Turning, she climbed into bed, wondering what she'd really learned about her life these few weeks.

She could stand up to her parents. She could choose the concerts and symphonies she wanted and let the others go. She could explore other types of music and leave New York and function just fine.

She might even have a choice in the future between performing and teaching—or maybe both.

She rolled over and pressed her hand against her chest, against the ache and fear that lodged in her heart that she was leaving the best thing that ever happened to her when she left Kirk Devon.

Kirk stepped back and looked at the sculpture. It was coming along. The drive to finish was strong. The curiosity about how it would look increased every day. The trees were about finished, and the face of the bluff. It was the figure poised at the top that would give the most trouble.

He tossed his tools down and went to the door, staring at the house next door. She was leaving tomorrow. He should have taken her to the festival, insisted on taking her home. The Tanners could have thanked her other ways. His grandfather would have found a way home or could have driven himself to begin with.

But he'd pulled back, trying to get used to the idea of never seeing her again. And after that amazing solo at the festival, he'd known she was more special than he thought. It had been enthralling. He wasn't sure he caught every note, but what he heard stirred emotions and memories.

Such genius should be shared with the world. She'd go on to greatness. He was humbled by her talent. Maybe she needed this summer break to see how far she'd come. Now she was returning and there was nothing he could do to change that. Nothing he would do. Her gift far surpassed Smoky Hollow.

His grandfather had done well at the festival. The ride back to the farm had been quiet. They'd done chores together, eaten supper. It was only when he was leaving that Hiram stopped him.

"Remember back when you were in school and studied American poets. One line always stuck with me—the saddest words are might have been. Think of what the future could be if we take the might have beens and made them the realities and not the way we think things should be."

Kirk thought about it. At the time he thought his grandfather was regretting lost opportunities. The years between his last performance and today's. But it could apply to lots of different things. Letting his wife go. Not spending more time helping neighbors. Letting his only son do a dangerous job which got him killed.

Or maybe he was trying to tell Kirk something more specific. What might have been if Angelica stayed. What would life be like, waking up with her every morning, going to bed together every night? Holding her, laughing with her, listening to her soft voice, straining to catch every nuance. Touching her. Kissing her. Teaching her about desire and passion and making love.

He leaned against the door post and considered everything. Life would never be the same once she left.

The next morning, Kirk headed for the cottage next door. Knocking, he waited. There was no answer. He opened the door and stepped inside, calling her name. Wandering into the kitchen, he saw it was spotless. Then a quick look in the other rooms showed the bed made, the music room as tidy as Webb Francis kept it. No priceless violin in sight.

She was gone.

He felt a flare of panic. She was really gone.

Heading for his truck, he made it to the store in record time.

Angelica stood on the porch talking with Paul and Melvin, her backpack on the floor, her precious violin case leaning against a post. Laughing at something one of the men said, she turned and saw him. In her hands, a teddy bear and pink hat.

Kirk stopped and stared at her for a long moment. One of the men must have said something because she turned to respond. As if in a dream, he climbed out of the truck and walked over.

"Come to tell her goodbye?" Paul asked.

"We said goodbye," Angelica said, flicking him a glance, then looking away.

Kirk studied her for a moment, trying to find some sign she'd be receptive to what he wanted to say.

The bus lumbered down the street, its engine noisy, the black smoke belching from the tailpipe.

She looked at the bus, back to Kirk.

He swallowed. Time was slipping by faster than he could deal with.

The bus stopped and the driver opened the door and stepped out.

"You going with me?" he asked.

She looked at the driver and nodded.

Kirk's heart sank.

"I only have the backpack and fiddle," she said, reaching over to scoop both up, balancing with the other items already in hand.

The bus driver took the backpack and climbed back into the bus.

She looked at Kirk, uncertainty filling her gaze.

"It was an amazing vacation. Thanks to you," she said with a sad smile. "Maybe I'll come visit again."

"If you leave, you'll never come back."

He knew that, but the words to keep her in Smoky Hollow wouldn't come. How could he ask her to give up all she'd spent a lifetime working for to settle in a backwater town like this?

"Maybe," she said.

She waved at the two on the porch, smiled again at Kirk, and stepped onto the bus. He remembered the day she stepped off that same bus. The uncertainty in her eyes. Today, it was reflected. He hadn't seen that look in weeks.

His voice wouldn't work. He wanted to ask her to stay. Yet the past interfered. His mother's defection, Alice's. He wasn't enough for a woman, he'd had ample proof. He couldn't utter a sound, only watch as she chose a seat by a window near him and waved again.

In seconds the bus was gone.

He stared after it a long time, gradually growing aware of the men behind him talking.

Turning, he raised an eyebrow in question.

"She said she got as much as she gave. That song she did yesterday was darn pretty."

Kirk nodded and walked to the truck. He had to remember that, her songs were for millions, not the few thousand people around his neck of the woods.

He started the engine but sat for a long moment staring down the now empty road.

"Be happy," he said, wondering what he could have done differently, to make her want to stay.

Chapter Twelve

The final notes sounded, fading softly from the concert hall. Angelica took a breath and lowered her violin. The bright lights blinded, but the applause was thunderous. She inclined her head in acknowledgment.

She smiled and bowed slightly again, wishing for the privacy of her Paris hotel room.

Staring out into the darkness beyond the bright lights illuminating the stage she couldn't help comparing it with the open-air stage in Bryceville.

She couldn't see anyone, not that she'd recognize anyone here. She smiled again and slowly walked off the stage. Another concert to check off. Only a couple of more and she'd be heading back to New York.

Once in the dressing area they'd assigned her, she quickly wiped her violin and placed it in the case. Congratulations and well wishes were called through the semi-open area where other musicians were talking, laughing and getting ready to leave. A couple looked grumpy, but she ignored them, wondering if they felt as lonely and uncertain as she herself did.

She touched the strings gently, remembering the sunshine and breeze when she'd played that song in Kentucky. What would the audience tonight have thought if she segued into Orange Blossom

Special after that Mozart piece? She shook her head. Maybe she should try it just once to see what happened. To see if she could purge the ache in her heart that had been steadfast since she left Smoky Hollow.

"These folks ever hear Orange Blossom Special?" a familiar voice asked behind her.

Angelica spun around, unable to believe her eyes. Was that truly Kirk Devon standing there—wearing a dark suit, brilliant white shirt and red power tie? He looked amazing. Her heart stuttered and then began beating furiously. She felt it take wing. Could he really be here in Paris? In this backstage area?

"Kirk?"

He nodded, his eyes watching her intently. She knew that look, had thought she'd never see it again. Her breathing had stopped. For a heartbeat time stood still. Then she forced herself to take a breath.

"What are you doing here?"

Her eyes searched every inch of that beloved face. She couldn't read him at all.

"I came to see you. Hear you."

"Could you—hear me, I mean?"

She never expected to see him again—especially not in Paris, France!

"Most of it, I think. Watching you was enough."

She stared at him, her heart racing.

"I didn't know you were coming to Paris."

"I didn't know myself until I bought my ticket. I went to New York to see you. But you weren't there."

"I've been on tour for several weeks."

"So I found out."

He stepped closer and pulled an envelope from his inside pocket.

"I brought you pictures of the sculpture. I told you I'd let you see it. Always keep my word. This seemed the best way."

For a moment she almost cried. He had come only to show her the finished art work? Trying desperately to gather her wits, she stared at the envelope. He held it out and she took it, almost snatching it away when she saw her fingers were trembling.

Opening it, she withdrew a half dozen photos. One was of the complete work, still on the floor of his studio. It looked amazing. She'd known it would. She looked at the next, a close-up of the trees, another a close-up of the cliff. The next—the woman on the edge. She stared at it for a long moment—it reflected yearning and hope with a hint of trepidation. How had he managed that with chisel and hammer? It was amazing.

She wanted to tell him so, but was afraid her voice wouldn't work. Her throat ached with tears. She'd longed to see him for weeks. Almost as if in answer to prayer he showed up and it was only to fulfill a promise to show her the carving.

"It's beautiful," she finally whispered, blinking to hold back tears.

"Almost as beautiful as its inspiration, eh?" he said slowly, stepping closer.

She looked up at that, tilting her head back to better see him as he drew near with each step.

"The thing is, Angelica, I got to thinking."

He stopped for a moment, licked his lips and took a breath.

"Ever since I can remember, Devon men can't keep their women. You know about my granddad and father. And me with Alice. I thought maybe there was something lacking in me."

"Nothing's lacking in you," she exclaimed involuntarily, hurt that he even thought such a thing.

"Maybe, maybe not. I've been a bit inflexible. Thought I knew exactly what I wanted. Only—seems like some things are worth bending for."

She frowned, not knowing where he was going.

"Like maybe spending my life outside of Smoky Hollow."

"But you love it there. You're an integral part of the community. What would your grandfather do if you left? Your neighbors?"

Was he serious? What did he mean?

"I expect they'll muddle along," he said, laughing softly and shaking his head. "I'm not the lynchpin of Smoky Hollow, and I do have a right to life on my terms."

He was close enough now he could reach out to brush back a tendril of hair, his fingers skimming her cheek.

She swallowed hard, holding her breath for fear of giving herself away. The commotion in the rest of the backstage area faded as she could only see Kirk. Was this how he focused when trying to hear? Did the rest of the world vanish?

"Am I enough, Angelica?"

"For what?" she asked, her knees threatening to give way.

Her heart pounded, blossoming with hope.

"For you to share a life with?"

She blinked, tears giving way.

"Oh, honey, don't cry. Please!" He wiped the tears with his thumb. "Would you marry me? Think about it before you answer. I'll go wherever you wish. We don't have to live in Smoky Hollow. I can carve wood anywhere there's space enough and light. I love you, Angelica. I never thought I'd fall in love like this. I know our family doesn't have a good track record with women, but I'll love you until the day I die and do my best to make you the happiest woman on the earth. But I can't go on without you. When you left, you took the sunshine with you. I thought a couple of times…

I mean, I hoped some of your reactions meant… Anyway, think about it, if you would."

She shook her head.

"Okay, just a thought." He looked around, as if noticing the others in the space. No one seemed to be paying them particular attention.

"No, no! I can't believe you think I need to spend a moment of consideration. I wanted you to ask me before I left. But you didn't."

He looked back at that. "You wanted me to ask? I almost did—at least to have you stay a little longer, let us explore this feeling. Only I was never sure you felt the same way. You're a bit naive and I thought you were experimenting. Only with me it went deeper. I love you like I've never loved anyone."

Her smile lit his world.

"I love you, Kirk. I think I have since we splashed in the creek together. I never had anyone to have fun with before."

"And I never knew."

Pulling her into his arms, he kissed her with all the pent up desire he'd had to deal with since August.

A few minutes later he pulled back. Both were breathing hard. Several musicians clapped and Angelica smiled up at him in confusion.

"Are you done here?" he asked.

"For tonight."

She smiled at the musicians and looked back at Kirk. Had she just dreamed this? If so, she wanted to never awaken.

"Then let's go for a late supper and talk. Explanations and plans. We've got a lifetime ahead of us to deal with."

She laughed. "I'm ready."

They found a small bistro, ordered a light supper and talked the night away. He explained his fear he couldn't offer her enough. She explained her hurt when he seemed to be so standoffish. They laughed as they remembered different incidents—from different viewpoints. Both agreed it had been a fantastic summer. One they could repeat for decades to come—knowing now they would spend those decades together.

"Let's get married in Paris," he said as they waited for the taxi that would take them to their hotels.

"Now?"

She looked up, stunned, then grinned.

"Why not?"

"It'll mean no big wedding and reception," he warned.

"You're the one with all the friends, if you don't care, I don't. I think it's a brilliant idea. Could we really?"

"We'll find out. So I take it the answer is yes? You never said," he said as a taxi swerved in toward the curb.

"Yes! I love you, Kirk Devon, and I always will. We can break the pattern of your family and be the first to live until we're old and gray and still loving each other."

He kissed her while the taxi driver patiently waited. It was Paris, after all.

Epilogue

Spring

The final curtain dropped and the musicians were able to leave their positions. Angelica carried her violin against her chest and hurried backstage. Her parents had come to hear the final symphony for the season and, of course, Kirk was waiting for her.

She went to her station backstage and was just placing it in its case when Kirk strode over, followed by her parents. He looked amazing in his tuxedo. Even better than he had in Paris last fall. Looking only at her, he walked straight through, others moving out of his way as if by magic. Her heart rate increased, and the smile that lit her face was involuntary. She couldn't help it, each time she saw him she fell in love all over again.

"Fantastic, Angel," he said, sweeping her into a hug and kissing her.

"Your best ever," her mother said, coming up and bustling around. "You were born to play music."

"Maybe," Angelica said. Privately she thought she was born to be Mrs. Kirk Devon, but she wasn't sure her mother wanted to hear that.

"You sure you won't come to Boston for a few days?" her father asked.

"No. Our plans are made. We're stopping in Atlanta to check on the gallery there and take stock of any statues unsold, then heading for home."

Her mother sniffed delicately.

"Home is here, Smoky Hollow is your vacation retreat."

Kirk stiffened and Angelica poked him gently. "Home is wherever we are, actually," she said. "But for the next few months, we'll be there."

Her mother gave Kirk a look that Angelica knew privately amused him. He'd won the most amazing prize, so he often said. He didn't care if her mother figuratively threw darts his way every time she saw him. She hadn't fully reconciled to the idea of her daughter married to a man who *whittled* for a living.

It was too early to prove to Kirk that their marriage would last forever. The past seven months had been fantastic. Dividing their time between New York for her engagements, and Smoky Hollow for down time, had proved the perfect solution. Even Kirk admitted he found inspiration in New York and they had bought a loft flat that would allow him all the light and space he needed to work. Now he had two studios and she had two homes.

Gradually the din eased as musicians left. They were having a late supper with her parents, then early in the morning heading south.

It was time to begin practicing for the music festival in Kentucky. Angelica had picked up quite a repertoire of folk songs. She loved her long weekends in Smoky Hollow, playing with Webb Francis and the children. Sam was getting better and better. Teresa Ann had her own violin now and could practice at home. But she still liked to practice with Angelica when she was in town.

Angelica couldn't wait to see them. And Hiram. He'd written in his last letter he had a brand new song to practice so they could perform together at the festival in August.

And tonight, after her parents left, she had some special news to share with her husband. She wondered if she should pull back from concerts and concentrate on building her family. Time enough to discuss that once he learned her news. She smiled up at Kirk as they walked out of the concert hall. Her breakaway summer had brought her happiness beyond her dreams. And there was no end in sight.